I0735694

S F
BOOKS

EDITOR-IN-CHIEF	CREATIVE DIRECTOR	MANAGING EDITOR	PRODUCTION ARTIST	MARKETING DIRECTOR
SEAN CLANCY	ALYSSA ALARCÓN SANTO	TYLER BERD	MAURA McGONAGLE	LUCAS WISEMAN

STAFF EDITOR	SPOT ILLUSTRATIONS AND GRAPHIC DESIGN BY	COVER AND ADDITIONAL SPOT ILLUSTRATIONS BY
ANNA CATALANO	ALYSSA ALARCÓN SANTO	MAURA McGONAGLE

COMIC BY LUCAS GUBALA | @BIRDHOUSEBOOKSTORE

Planet Scumm is a triannual short fiction anthology. Visit **planetscumm.space** for submissions.

First Printing, 2023   ISBN: 978-1-970154-88-7

© SPARK & FIZZ BOOKS
Portland | Boston | Hell

SPARK & FIZZ BOOKS PRESENTS

PLANET SCUMM

SPRING 2023   "ARCANA MAJOR"   ISSUE NO. 15

— A STARCROSSED TABLE OF CONTENTS —

VII
THE CHARIOT

The story of my time with *Planet Scumm* begins, as so many stories do, with *Jeff Wayne's Musical Version of the War of the Worlds*.

Well... "begins" is strong. The *actual* official beginning of my time on Scummy's crew came when Ty Berd called me up one day to say, "Heya, Sean old buddy! Wanna make a sci-fi mag?" My response in the affirmative was probably equally cinematic.

That said, certainly the most *memorable* event from those early Scumm days came when the two of us gathered in my apartment in Boston to put together our very first issue, with Jeff Wayne's masterpiece as our backing music. Lacking any better method of binding books, and also lacking any common sense, we commenced assembly on that inaugural *Planet Scumm* by jamming staples into the rough center of a sheaf of 11"x17", then hammering the whole thing over the centerfold. Like, actually hammering, with a hammer from my tool cabinet.

In my memory, track five from the album is always playing—"Thunder Child."

For those unfamiliar with *Jeff Wayne's Musical Version of the War of the Worlds* (or... H.G. Welles' *The War of the Worlds*), "Thunder Child" describes the ironclad HMS *Thunder Child* as she and her crew defend a human flotilla from a trio of martian "fighting machines."

It's easy to romanticize that moment, and to imagine that Ty and I were hammering together the metal plating on our very own HMS *Thunder Child* in *Planet Scumm*—creating something loud and aggressive and honest, but also archaic, and an underdog in a world radically altered by terrestrial machines of a different sort than the martians'.

One of my main goals while editing *Planet Scumm* these past six years has been to fuse some of that bubble-helmeted, ray-gun-toting sci-fi spirit of old with the new ideas and writers of today. Scummy, our mascot, is a curious throwback consisting of equal parts Wolfman Jack and the Blob. He's a monster, but he's a *straightforward* monster, damn it (not to mention a useful mouthpiece for an EIC who loathes writing an earnest "letter from the editor").

It's hard to imagine Scummy getting *too* choked up about my departure, so I won't either.

Instead, I'd like to focus on how much the magazine has grown in the past six years, and how much it will continue to grow with our current team. It seems like every issue we're breaking some other record for the mag, be it our submission count, our word count, our pay rate, or some other milestone. And beyond those accomplishments, we have some really exciting projects in the pipeline that will expand *Planet Scumm* beyond short fiction. I'd tell you, but I'm legally prohibited from disclosing any details. (And no, it's not ScummCoin. It MAY be *Planet Scumm 3D*.)

Two final things to get off my chest before I head out the airlock here. First: my thanks. Thanks to Eric Loucks, Ty Berd, Sam Rheaume, Greg Bergeron, Andrew Chevenert, Alyssa Alarcón Santo, Maura McGonagle, Anna Catalano, Lucas Wiseman, and all the writers and readers who make up the extended Scumm Family.

Second: my recommendation. Go listen to *Jeff Wayne's Musical Version of the War of the Worlds*. It's really good!

ROLL ON THUNDER CHILD

ARTWORK BY SAM RHEAUME, FROM ISSUE #10, "SUPERGIANT-X"

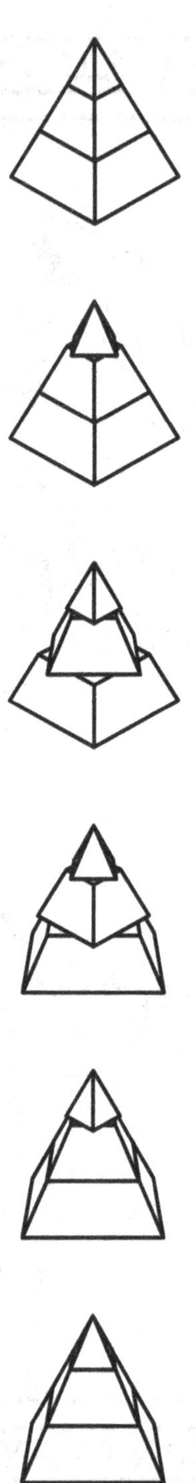

PLANET SCUMM ISSUE #15
ARCANA MAJOR

AUTHOR BIOS

RENAN BERNARDO is a science fiction and fantasy writer from Rio de Janeiro, Brazil. His fiction has appeared in *Apex Magazine, Podcastle, Solarpunk Magazine,* and elsewhere. He was among the authors selected for the 2021 Imagine 2200 climate-fiction contest. In Brazil, he was a finalist for two important SFF awards and published multiple stories. His fiction has been published in multiple languages, including German, Italian, Japanese, and Portuguese. Find him on Twitter at @RenanBernardo and his website at renanbernardo.com.

I wrote the first version of "The Throat of San Dante" years ago for a Norwegian story contest. For a long time, I thought about a mutating metropolis where buildings, parks, and streets change all the time. How would someone be able to live in a place like this? Why did it exist at all? San Dante prioritizes whatever generates the most profit. No life comes first. But what drives the story is the people—Rita and her aunt—and the way they are swallowed by their own city.

YANG-YANG WANG is a writer living in the Seattle area. His fiction has appeared in magazines such as *Lightspeed* and he's written for games like *Magic: The Gathering, ZEPHON,* and a forthcoming MOBA from PlayGig. He serves on the board of Clarion West and the Carl Brandon Society steering committee.

"After Meal" was written during his second week at Clarion West.

AI JIANG is a Chinese-Canadian writer and an immigrant from Fujian. She is a member of the HWA, SFWA, and Codex. Her work can be found in *The Magazine of Fantasy & Science Fiction, The Dark and Uncanny,* and many other publications. She is the holder of Odyssey Workshop's 2022 Fresh Voices Scholarship. Her debut novella (April 2023) is forthcoming with Dark Matter INK. Find her on Twitter at @AiJiang_) and online at aijiang.ca.

I had the idea for "Cover Your Eyes" while I was brewing on how society can look the other way in the face of rising challenges, and how governments or the media might distort facts, convincing citizens to believe in a fabricated reality.

REBECCA CAMPBELL is a Canadian writer whose short fiction has won the Sunburst Award and the Theodore Sturgeon Memorial Award. In 2022, she published two novellas: *The Talosite* (Undertow Publications) and *Arboreality* (Stelliform Press). *Arboreality* was nominated

AUTHOR BIOS

for a Philip K. Dick Award. *The Talosite* is on the Stoker Award preliminary ballot. You can find her online at whereishere.ca

I wrote "Such Thoughts Are Unproductive" because I wanted to explore the intimate consequences of totalitarianism and state surveillance—things that viscerally terrify me—in a near-future version of my own country. In some ways, I continue to find this story more disturbing than the graphic body horror I've written.

CHINAZA EZIAGHIGHALA is a physician who moonlights as a storyteller. An alumn of the University of Iowa's International Writing Program, she is published in the British Science Fiction Association's *Fission II Vol. 1* anthology, *Mythaxis* and *Brittle Paper*. CHIMERA, her debut novella, is forthcoming from Nosetouch Press in 2024. Connect with her at chinazaeziaghighala.disha.page or on Twitter at @chinazaezims.

"A Dose of Insight" is a play on words on empathy as a doctor's prescription and how the character swallows his pill the hard way.

JAMES STODDARD has had short fiction appear in publications such as *Amazing Stories* and *The Magazine of Fantasy and Science Fiction*. His short stories, "The Battle of York," and "The First Editions," appeared respectively in *The Year's Best SF 10*, published by Eos Books, and *The Year's Best Fantasy 9* from Tor. His novel, *The High House*, won the Compton Crook Award for best fantasy by a new novelist and was also nominated for several other awards.

"The Battle of York" was inspired by Scottish poet James Macpherson's Ossian—which he either "discovered" or invented, depending on what you believe—and the short story, "Letter from a Higher Critic," by Stewart Robb, in which a scholar "proves" that World War II never happened.

KARINA DOVE ESCOBAR (she/they) is a new writer from New Jersey and Connecticut, who now lives in New Mexico. She often describes the process of writing stories as both a playground and a medicine.

In this story, the playground was a daydream about the two halves of evolution... the realm of our ancestors, the realm of our descendents. The medicine helped me face certain anxieties about the many ways our short-sightedness could cost us.

YUME KITASEI (yumekitasei.com) is a Brooklyn-based Japanese and American writer of speculative fiction. Her stories

AUTHOR BIOS

have appeared in such publications as *New England Review*, *Catapult*, and *Nashville Review*. Her debut novel, *The Deep Sky*, is forthcoming from Flatiron Books in 2023.

"Ghosts in the Ash" is at its heart a diaspora story.

GEOFFREY W. COLE's award-winning short fiction has appeared in such publications as *Clarkesworld*, *EscapePod*, and *Imaginarium: The Year's Best Canadian Speculative Writing*. He is the 2016 winner of the Premis Ictineu for best story translated into Catalan. He lives with his wonderful wife, three sons, and giant hound outside Toronto, Canada. Visit Geoff at geoffreywcole.com.

Over the years, I've worked many jobs, including Segway tour leader, creek engineer, and golf course locker room attendant. Only one of those jobs was as wretched as the career Marjormam faces in "The Way of the Shrike," but the choice Marjormam is confronted with, between her art and her day job, is one I've been balancing my entire life. I think she chooses well.

SPECIAL THANKS TO OUR TEAM OF FIRST READERS:

Our sturdy crew of volunteers is what makes the Scumm so virulent and phosphorescent. Send a note over to us at planetscummsubmissions@gmail.com if you're interested in joining our elite literary task force.

- **JAMES ABYS-SMITH** feeds within the sinews of corporations and government.

- **A. KATHERINE BLACK** survives on a diet of monster movies and coffee.

- **KATRINA CARRUTH** is a chaotic-neutral chef.

- **MATT LARGO** lives and works in Boston.

- **NOAH LEMELSON** is a featherless biped.

- **LOGAN MARROW** is a tortured genius from the Hudson Valley.

- **ISEULT MURPHY** is a piece of space debris that occasionally writes horror stories.

- **SAM REBELEIN** is currently writing his fifth short story about creepy clowns.

- **PAUL C.K. SPEARS** is a UFO-hunting coffee enthusiast.

- **DAN STINTZI** is a fan of skeletons.

- **DALE STROMBERG** is two beers away from comfy.

XVI
THE TOWER

Nanofacturers transform the city of San Dante outside my loft's window.

My hands ebb and flow, swiftly adjusting blocks on the holo-pad, shaping my art, imitating the city outside. I don't know how far I can go this time before my hands betray me. My eyes shift between the art and the changing city block, grasping some details, overlooking others. As the skyscrapers in front of me coalesce in new forms and sizes, I move holo-parts to their most suitable positions, as if I have any power over the reshaping. My fingers dance at only a fraction of the city nanofacturers' speed, positioning windows and balconies in small-scale holographic art.

My fingers hurt. I bite my dry lips, tasting and swallowing iron.

Not this time. I've never come this far. It's working now.

The only way I can make my art is in a frenzy, thrusting body and mind beyond fatigue, flowing with the real city outside the best I can. If I don't rush to follow the city's reshaping, my hands will fail, and creativity will vanish.

The tail of the mermaid tattooed on my left arm flashes. I catch a glimpse of the notification but don't read it. I know what it says:

Rita, buildings and parks in your district are currently undergoing economic reshaping. Please, be aware of address changes and keep your distance from the affected streets.

The back of my mind reminds me that I have to speak with Aunt Maggie, but I shove it back.

No distractions. Mind and body belong to the art right now.

San Dante unveils the many streets and alleys around the buildings, black waves of graphene-asphalt rippling between the high-rises. Sweat beads on my forehead, but I go on. The rhythm can't dwindle now.

Hands swirling, sliding, sweeping holo-parts, squeezing and flattening them as needed, distributing my little roads throughout the holographic San Dante. One with the rising tide of stone and metal, singing its fast song of diamond-nanotubes, polymers, and rock.

My fingers stiffen.

I try to move my hands, forcing them to shape, but the muscles are like rusty gearwheels. I let them fall on my lap, anger coursing through my body. The holo-art of San Dante flickers. The table-projected keyboard of the holo-pad blinks, waiting for input.

Outside, the real city block wraps up its terraces, penthouses, and rooftops, economic algorithms fueling the nanofacturers, driving the tiny black cubes to draw the block anew. Within days, the new offices will be swarming with new businesses and executives energized by coffee.

"Damn!"

I raise my hands and stare at my shivering fingers, and the whitened scars webbing around them. They twinge from time to time since I was a kid, like a weight pulling my hands down, hindering my art.

I close my eyes and sigh, dropping my hands on the table.

The voice and blurred images that often complete my pain flood me. The sound is soft and frail, about to fracture into small pieces and fade away. I can't distinguish what it says—I never can—but it soothes me. Giggles come from inside these shards of remembrance, and a light twinkles nearby. My mother. I never saw her, she died too early in my life, but it's her. And her ghost presence in my thoughts is medicine for the cramps, as if she's there to comfort me the way nobody ever did.

I stretch my fingers with ease now, but it's too late. My art remains unfinished in front of me, half-buildings wavering in incomplete gradients. Yellow, blue, pink—more colorful than the grays of the block outside, now changed into new hotels, offices, and empty apartments.

My tattoo blinks. The reminder: *Tell Aunt Maggie about district alterations.*

She never sees San Dante's notifications. I read the attached statement from the city:

Hi Rita,

San Dante requires that you move. Your whole district will undergo an extreme economic reshaping in fifteen days. Most of its buildings are going to change for economic adjustments.

It will not be safe to stay. San Dante recommends you move to one of the newly established areas in the outskirts of the city. Your city and your society thank you! Your account will be credited for the trouble.

I double tap my arm to dismiss it.

It's been thirteen days since the notification. Maybe the moment Aunt Maggie has been talking about for so long has arrived, that metaphor she clings to about slipping into the throat of San Dante.

It won't be easy to convince Aunt Maggie to move. But it won't be harder than visiting her in her darkness and dust.

☆ ☆ ☆

The blinds are all shut tight. The corners where light is supposed to find its way in are blocked with cardboard. The only lamp in the ceiling is dimmed by a coat of dirt, but Aunt Maggie doesn't seem to notice or care. Apart from the lighting, everything seems unchanged since I left.

"I live here legally, Rita."

Aunt Maggie dusts the overused dresser she'd put in the living room. In a city that might change so suddenly, she's unable to let go of sundries and heavy furniture. The dresser is cluttered with small chests for earrings and necklaces. The most flowery ones were for my jewelry. But they are empty now, some with their lids broken. Aunt Maggie doesn't use jewelry anymore, only a gray dress, frayed at its edges.

"San Dante won't take away my home." Aunt Maggie's reflection moves in the mirror of the dresser, an unrecognizable, distorted smear, amplifying the jagged scar on her left cheek.

The finish of the glass was already matte when I started to shave my head, crouched for the best view of my scalp. Aunt Maggie

pulled me up and told me I should straighten my back if I intended to take care of people in hospitals or manage profitable companies. I argued that the mirror was broken, but she never cared. A girl should find her way with what she has at her disposal.

And I did—I still do.

I can't find the courage to sit on The Couch though.

Sit there, girly girl, you might want to learn some lessons.

The mildew may grow arms to trap me there, making me listen to my aunt's reprimands forever. Still, I try to argue.

"That's not the way the city works. Every citizen must heed the official instructions."

"Oh, must we?" Aunt Maggie dusts a lampshade which has been crooked for a long time. Dust puffs out of it. "We live in a dictatorship?"

"All civil works in the whole country are performed by the nanofacturers."

I'm waiting for the cleaning to end, careful not to touch The Couch. "It's the only way to maintain a stable economy... or so people say. The nanofacturers won't just stop when you're in their path."

"You don't need to explain it to me. I know my Dante better than you." She turns to face me, the duster in her hands like a weapon. "In my time, AIs were just silly. You know? Robots to make us laugh, to help us find our way in the streets. Not to transform everything. Your mother would agree with me on this. I think she would. She was smart, if anything."

My fingers twinge. When Aunt Maggie brings up my mother, it's to upset me.

I turn to the ancient wood door. It's the best part of her house. It's discolored and swollen by humidity, but it's still the only way out—the path I trod years ago full of expectations. The path to a world of light where I hoped to find liberty in holo-carving, but instead found only hand cramps and a strange, self-abusive longing for the aunt I'd left behind.

"Wait, girl." Aunt Maggie touches my elbow. For a moment, it's delicate, but then her fingers put some pressure on it. Not too much, just enough to show who's still in charge. "I made lunch for us."

"You made lunch?"

She never made anything for me after I turned eighteen, decided to study holo-art, and left her den.

No answer. She disappears into the kitchen. Cabinet doors squeal.

My hands rest on the dull doorknob that was once golden. The air sticks in my chest, though my heart is pounding fast. It's my time to leave. She's been warned. She knows what to do to survive the economic reshaping. She'll just gather the few useful belongings she has in here and leave.

I turn the doorknob.

The smell of goulash wafts into the living room. "I found a holo-pad from your mother."

I turn away from the door and gasp. "I thought you had nothing from her."

Aunt Maggie appears in the hallway carrying a bowl of goulash, a silhouette looming in the living room. "*Almost nothing. I have her holo-pad, though. You might want to take a look.*"

I sit down at the table in the same chair where, as a kid, I was told that I should always eat with my mouth closed, and never, ever disrespect an older person. That's the place where I learned that some things in life have prices, and if you break a plate you have to pay for it—even if that price is throwing your holo-pad out the window.

That's the place where I daydreamed, and where I discovered that holo-carving models of buildings was my thing, not abstract sculptures like so many other artists preferred. And that's where my hands first betrayed me.

Most important of all things, it's *my* chair, and it's safer than The Couch.

Sit there, Rita. You stay there until sundown, and never bring this twinkling pad in here again.

There's no mildew in the chair, or at least not enough to engulf me.

Aunt Maggie sets the table for lunch, though in the dim light it seems like it's dinner. The goulash cools in the center of the table, and an obsolete, inactive holo-pad Aunt Maggie brought from her you-shall-never-enter bedroom stands next to her empty plate.

My eyes fix on it. Its keys are physical, not surface-projected ones. The art will have a lower resolution. It's rare today, sort of vintage. But none of it really matters because it's the first item I've ever seen that belonged to my mother. Aunt Maggie sits at the table and glares at me.

"Can I turn it on?" I say.

"Let's eat first."

So we eat, though I'm not hungry. The goulash is just fine, saltier than the way I remember. Silence fills the living room, occasionally broken by the spoons clinking on the plates. I try to talk about the nanofacturers, the economic reshaping, and how every citizen and company is responsible for their own stuff. Aunt Maggie's answers are exactly what I expect, monosyllables and nods. When her plate is almost empty—and I know she'll stand up before I finish mine—I look at her.

She knows what I want and shrugs, facing the remainders of her goulash, scratching her scar with overgrown nails.

"It's old, maybe broken."

I grab the holo-pad, scanning her face for disapproval. I find nothing.

My mother touched this. It's the closest I've ever been to her.

It's a limited edition, fabricated for public institutions. It has tiny initials of the Ministry of Civil Engineering protruding out of its base. Holo-carving isn't an activity restricted to artists. Engineers and architects also use holo-pads to make their designs. I swivel it around and catch every dent and scratch, everything that made this my mother's item.

"If you hate holo-art, why didn't you throw it away?" I put the holo-pad on the middle of the table.

"Don't know. Finish your goulash."

"I'll turn it on."

Before I do anything, Aunt Maggie extends her arm and presses the power button. A yellow tube glimmers in the air, catching the dust floating in the apartment. I hold my breath. Aunt Maggie seems to hold hers too. The tube swirls.

Loading.

My heart stops in my chest, and my stomach roils with the goulash.

Loading.

It seems it will never end. Maybe the holo-pad is broken after all this time in Aunt Maggie's bedroom.

Then, it lights up.

It's a crude building, yellowish as the loading tube, not unlike most buildings in San Dante, but crowned with an imposing tree that had been intricately hewn into the model. It's not a technical carving for engineering projects. It doesn't have annotations or calculations appended to it. It's pure holo-art.

I touch the holography and the building flickers into an amorphous shape, ready to vanish. I recoil and it comes back to normal. The art of my mother amazes me so much that I stay silent. I remember how my aunt despised me when she found me in my bedroom with a holo-pad.

She was a sturdy woman then, but when she saw me holo-carving for the first time, just a child crawling into preteens, she transformed into a beast. *How dare you bring this thing into my house?*

"Tell me about my mother," I say, dust floating through the holo-building, the last vestige of my mom in the whole world besides my aunt's memory. "You never told me anything about her. Did she holo-carve buildings like me?"

"She worked for the Ministry of Civil Engineering."

"That I know. Who was she? How did she die?" My fingers hurt. I clench my teeth.

"She valued this art more than... people."

"Why? Tell me everything, it's my right to know. I'm not a child anymore."

"You're a child." She hits the power button on the holo-pad, and the building flickers off. "I've tried to turn you into a real woman, but you left me. So you're a child."

I stand up. "You won't tell me, will you?"

Aunt Maggie glowers at me, but for the first time she seems about to break.

"Go away," she says.

I blink, not wanting to let the tears muffle my thoughts. I stalk to the door and touch the doorknob, but come back for the holo-pad. Aunt Maggie presses it down on the table.

"It's mine." I grit my teeth.

Aunt Maggie's hand shudders, but she lets it go.

Aunt Maggie is crying, but I couldn't care less about her now. She is a person full of secrets and problems, hard to figure out. I open the door. The chilly air outside and the lights of the corridor invade the apartment. They're welcoming. With the holo-pad clutched in my armpit, I turn to her one more time.

"Don't forget. Economic reshaping two days from now." I bite my lips. "Please, don't stay."

She flinches. "Your mother didn't want you." Her voice echoes in the corridor.

My legs tremble, tears stream down my cheeks. My hands are about to explode, the joints stuck.

I don't turn back.

She's lying. She's just a liar.

☆ ☆ ☆

My mother's holo-pad is in front of me on the table. I'm afraid to turn it on. What can I find in her art, in that tawny flickering building? Can I see the desire to leave me behind?

She valued this art more than... people.

I close my hands in fists and press them against the cafeteria table from where I am watching my district, waiting for the economic reshaping. A twinge bolts across my fingers. I don't even know where my scars come from. Aunt Maggie says it was a domestic accident when I was too small to remember. She always refused to delve into the details.

Ultra-fast buses bolt along the sidewalks, an instantaneous silvery flicker. An electronic odor whiffs into the cafeteria. Cars hover in the smoothly asphalted streets of San Dante, an infinitude of driverless chrome carrying passengers out of my district before the economic reshaping starts. Around me, people anticipate the nanofacturers' show, talking and setting their cam-lenses to register the changes.

And Aunt Maggie is there, somewhere, ready to slip into the throat of San Dante.

I flip the holo-pad and rub my finger on the Ministry of Civil Engineering's initials on its base, as if the dusty lint gathered on it can provide any answers. All research I've done on my past turned out blank. It was as if I just popped into existence out of nowhere into a gloomy apartment with an aunt that never opened her mouth to talk about the past.

I close my eyes. My joints relax.

That voice echoes in my mind, about to break itself. It's my mother, the woman who didn't want me. Someone giggles, lights twinkle, and—

Yellow lights.

I pry my eyes open and turn the holo-pad on. While the tube swirls and the art loads, a twinge curls in my stomach.

The building flickers on. That's it.

I thrust my hands through it, turning it into a distorted shape.

Giggles. More than one. We'd giggled together, mother and daughter.

My tattoo blinks: *Some buildings and parks in your district will undergo severe economic reshaping. Please, keep your distance.* I double tap my arm.

An almost indistinct hum starts and the ground shakes, very slightly, as if some machinery had been turned on in the cafeteria. But it's the nanofacturers getting ready to reshape my district. And among dust and closed blinds my aunt will fall into the city's throat.

Liar. We giggled together. My mother did want me.

"It's changing now," says a nearby voice.

Nanofacturers heap up around the district, lifting barriers to close the streets. They don't wait for the barriers though. The tiny robots swarm on like millions of spiders clustered together, emerging from the pavement. Double-hung windows are converted from stone and wood into glass, apartment buildings slowly acquire the features of offices.

Walls rise, walls fall. The pavement gobbles lampposts, hydrants, traffic lights, even cars and objects left behind.

I turn the holo-pad off and tuck it into my backpack. It's time to go to my new place in the outskirts of San Dante. People love the show, but I always think of it as a sad one. It's like paying the economic stability price with memories.

"Set your cam-lenses..." someone says.

"It's okay, everyone is safe..."

Aunt Maggie isn't.

Tears well up in my eyes. Perhaps she's there eating one last goulash, dust finding its place for the last time in her furniture. Maybe the mildew is outstretching its infinitesimal branches for one last attempt to dominate The Couch. Within a few hours, my home may be the kitchen of a new modern place that will bring happiness and sadness to another family. Built upon my memories, even though they're far from happy.

"I told you, dear. Everyone is safe..."

All will be fine, you're safe now, my mother had told me. Her voice had been cracked and teary. *You're safe now.*

Safe from what? From her thoughts of abandonment? I remember jabbing my little fingers into her holo-art, a building peaked by a lonely tree. It flickered. And we giggled.

All will be fine.

And my mother stood and walked to the door to check on something. Tiptoeing. She slowly opened the door and looked outside, as if making sure someone else wouldn't come back. It was an ancient wooden door with a golden doorknob.

I'm sorry, Rita.

Sniffing and tears. Not my mother. The woman who soothed me and giggled with me had a bandage on her left cheek.

"It can't be..." I stand up, snatching my backpack. "Aunt Maggie..."

My tears blur the sight of the morphing buildings in the district. I run.

☆ ☆ ☆

The district whirs. Nanofacturers ripple through the pavement, swallowing everything in sight—repainting stores, banks, diners. In minutes, the restaurant where I first had lunch after moving from Aunt Maggie's house mutates into a convention center, its windows transforming into double doors, the new design dripping over the old one. It's like they'd never been there at all.

You're in danger! my tattoo alerts, the mermaid's tail flashing red. *Please, stay outside the barriers.*

I double tap my arm.

I dart up the stairs of Aunt Maggie's apartment building, panting, the backpack flapping. All around me, hidden in the walls somewhere, nanofacturers buzz. Aunt Maggie is a part of her apartment. She would never leave it.

If you want to go, you're free, girl. You're eighteen now. But remember, you have no one else.

I didn't at the time, and Aunt Maggie doesn't now.

I pry open the door, winded. Nothing has changed. The blinds are shut tight with cardboard. The dust clouds in the air. And the remainders of our dinner lay on the table with flies encircling it.

You're in danger!

I double slap my arm and dismiss the notification.

"Aunt Maggie!" I manage to yell.

The only response is the nanofacturers' hum. What if she decided to leave? I'm the fool here. My aunt is safe somewhere. That's why the table is still set. She just ran away.

"Rita."

I turn back. *Aunt Maggie.*

My body tenses up, my hands twitch. Nanofacturers rattle nearby, perhaps in the level below or climbing the stairs to make me slip into the throat we're all going to slip into someday.

"It was you..." I say. "Me, the... the holo-pad, and you."

"I planned to tell you in our lunch, but I couldn't," Aunt Maggie says, one hand gripping The Couch. Red circles surround her eyes.

She makes an effort to speak, her lips grim lines. Behind her, the hum is becoming a rumble.

"I had to get rid of her."

Her face scrunches in pain, every word a groan. She clasps her left cheek, completely covering her scar as if wanting to hold something in place.

"What—"

"My sister... Your mother. She beat me since our childhood... badly. I ripped you from her a few weeks after she hurt your... hands. She tried to hit me, but instead..." Aunt Maggie shakes her head. "So I sent her away."

I raise my hands and scowl at them. There's a burning through all my body. The hum is intense. We won't be able to hear each other in a few minutes.

From memories that have been sequestered in the corners of my mind, I recall an intense fight. Two people screaming... Shiny particles—*shards of glass*—slithering through my hands... The flash of pain...

I shudder and pinch my lips.

"I'm sorry," Aunt Maggie says. "I made you grow up without your mother."

You're in danger! You're in danger! The mermaid tail repeatedly flashes in red and purple.

Aunt Maggie closes her eyes. I can see her searching for something that was always there inside her, cloaked by her disgust, crusted by her wounds. Finally, she speaks.

"You look like her..." Then, with her nails jabbing The Couch, words sputter out of her mouth, certain that the end is coming, that we're slipping, "An artist, holo-buildings carver, same cheeks, same way of looking at me, that fierceness that one day might raise a fist and—"

She shakes her head.

"You... You hid it all from me," I stammer. "Why? You could've told me, you could've counted on me for—"

Aunt Maggie raises a hand, glancing behind at the distorted mass bulging out from the corridor like a solid, black wave. Her eyes brim with tears and she opens her mouth to let it all out, before the end.

It's her way of slipping.

"Half of me wanted you to leave, to go find your mother. The other half wanted you to stay even though I felt like a farce. A thief."

Nanofacturers overrun the apartment. It begins to change. The ancient door turns into a glassed panel. I hurl myself forward and pull Aunt Maggie closer.

"I'm sorry," she says into my ear.

The Couch vanishes under the nanofacturers, and blue, clean carpet stretches across the living room. The table with our last meal disappears. There's nothing else to do but accept the newness.

"You did what was right," I say, but I'm not sure if Aunt Maggie can hear me now, even this close. "You were there with me all the time. You're here now."

I enfold her in my arms. She doesn't move, her body stiff, her arms tight and inflexible against her sides. The nanofacturers encircle us, whirring, spreading a magnificent cerulean-tinted linoleum. I continue to hold Aunt Maggie tight. She raises her arms and clumsily passes them around my shoulders.

At least here, in the end, we are what we never were before. We're family.

The nanofacturers begin to climb our shoes and legs, a thousand needles finding their way up—

And then they stop.

The nanofacturers slide across the floor, turned off. They fall from my legs and splay around my shoes. The whirring stops. From inside my backpack, the holo-pad beeps incessantly.

"The failsafe for Ministry employees..." Aunt Maggie mutters. "I took—stole it—from your mother."

And I had taken it from Aunt Maggie. If I hadn't come back with it, the nanofacturers would have killed her. I shake all throughout.

"You're with me," I repeat, in case she didn't hear me before. "I'm with you, Aunt Maggie. We're safe."

The place around us has become a shining apartment. All that remains of our lives is the dusty dresser and a few flowery broken lids. And us.

KNIGHT
OF SWORDS

The Kel'Thuzz die screaming like wind chimes in a gentle breeze. The stifling air of planet Kel 5 shimmers gently with their cries, a rippling curtain that distorts the shapes of my fellow Earthforce soldiers.

The violet sand dunes of Kel 5 are no longer a battlefield, but a buffet of the vanquished. Discarded EF armors, thick-plated gunmetal decorated like a knight's tale, dot the landscape as their wearers engage in a hungry reaping under the ruby sun.

The soldier closest to me falls upon a prone Kel'Thuzz defender, smashing the alien's crystalline symmetry with his axe. The alien doesn't fight back as pieces fall off its meter-long body with each hack, littering the ground with shards that pulse gently, and blood like a radiant kaleidoscope.

If there is an intelligent designer to the universe, then it certainly has a sense of humor. How could we have prepared for humanity's first contact to be with aliens whose deaths reward our every sense?

Their mortal shrieks are sweet melodies, their bodies shatter into precious gems, and their blood spills like beams of vivid rainbow. But none of that compares to eating them.

The marine squats among the still-resonating pieces, his face warped like a twisted canvas as he picks the shards up. His eyes roll back and jubilation rumbles in his throat as the morsels of Kel'Thuzz disappear down his gullet.

Bumps rise on my skin despite the heat.

I'm mesmerized by the sight of his head thrown back, eyes unfocused, and the flecks of violet sand around his mouth and in his beard. He's no longer a soldier, but something primal and honest and long forgotten.

He is an insatiable mouth, a gaping portal to the abyss, awaiting satisfaction.

He is me five months ago, lost to the same hunger.

Saliva floods my mouth in response to the memory of eating the aliens. An electric serpent jolts down my spine, and for a moment there is the smell of Earth and lightning as my bloodless fist tightens on my knife handle.

And I need a patch.

I pull out a Meal Ready-to-Eat bar. I slam its thick plastic coating into my thigh like a shot of Naloxone. The impact brings me back, away from the savage and back to the soldier. My knife stabs into the MRE packaging—once, twice, then three times before its tip finds purchase in the opaque hard-shell.

A sudden pressure relieves, not in the package but in me, as I tear the ration bar open. I close my eyes and focus everything onto the fist-length bar as I take my first bite.

The MRE tastes like the devil's shit-covered balls. The concentrated sodium melts on my tongue like flavored napalm. It spreads to coat the inside of my mouth, searing my taste buds and burning out all hope of sweet and sour and savory. But the scent of dying aliens leaks through in a stream of orange-lime rosemary, so I take a second bite, then a third, and then more.

My mouth battles my desire to relapse. My teeth churn up the MRE bar like an oscillating piston. The brittle, off-white surface breaks into jagged bits and nutrient dust between my jaws. I chew with such violent purpose that each crunch is like the shattering of icebergs and the brushing of continents. The aftershocks rumble through my cheeks and up my ears, and the apex of each reverberation is a short prayer drowning out the sounds of my battalion feasting around me.

Pieces of the MRE sneak themselves between my teeth or leave stinging lines in their wake, and the hint of warm iron flavors my salt-saliva cocktail. The taste of my blood is as comforting as a scalding shower after a long murder, and I savor every bit of punishment as I take the remaining bite.

I chew the last piece of jagged sodium with a desperate relish, rejoicing as the burn spreads beyond my throat and up my nose and into my brainstem, where it goes beyond sweet and sour and savory to finally destroy the bitterness. With no sense of taste left, I regain my breath.

But it's no use. The orgy of victorious consumption hits my senses again, and the memories crash through the wall of drying saline left by the MRE with all the gentleness of a drop ship crash.

My first taste of Kel'Thuzz was like Bacchus manifest.

Anyone who's ever had a bite experiences gentle hexahedrons at the back of your mouth and the front of your mind, their cold angles melting as fast as your thoughts touch them, only to suffuse down your throat and into a tight glow in your stomach. Their alien bodies aren't so much food, to be broken down into proteins and fats and carbohydrates, but euphoria and light and immortality coalescent.

Their taste was the answer to a question I'd always been asking, and I got lost in the cycle of eating and killing, killing then eating, then eating and eating and eating and eating...

I grope for my last MRE as I'm drawn towards the soldiers and the shards and the desire to fill the hunger that gnaws the space between my stomach and my heart. I can't find it though, or I don't want to find it, and my grasping hands reach forward instead, desperate for anything to save me.

The soldier hardly reacts as I grab the collar on his pressure-suit and shove him to the ground. He's still lost in the dream of his appetite, even though the Kel'Thuzz next to him is nothing but chips and glitter on the purple dunes.

I pull my squad mate up with one hand and into a sitting position. He fights me bitterly—his axe is too far away, but not his fists or feet or teeth. My cheekbone splits as he repeatedly strikes it, but I hold on. He gags as I force two fingers into the back of his mouth. The air sours as streams of light spill onto the ground. His head sags as he falls, weary from our fight and the sudden emptying of his stomach.

It's almost thirty minutes before his eyes refocus and his sweat subsides. I find my last MRE and hold it out in front of his face. My bruised jaw hurts as I yell at him to take a bite. He does so, snarling, half-aware of me but mostly aware of the subsiding pleasure of eating. As he takes a second bite, I see his hands twitch and his eyes glance towards a half-eaten Kel'Thuzz in the distance. I know what he's thinking, but he makes no move towards it.

I lift him to his feet and we look at our battalion around us, still deep in the throes of their butchery. The soldier grips my shoulder as he points to a man far in the distance.

Save my brother, he implores. I shove the soldier towards his brother.

Save him yourself, I yell.

The soldier stares at me and spits on the ground. His saliva still glows as I watch him stumble between Kel'Thuzz corpses. His steps linger and for a heartbeat, I don't know if he'll make it. Then he pushes on until he, too, is a shimmer among tinkling songs and pulsing fragments.

I move to the next marine.

IX
OF SWORDS

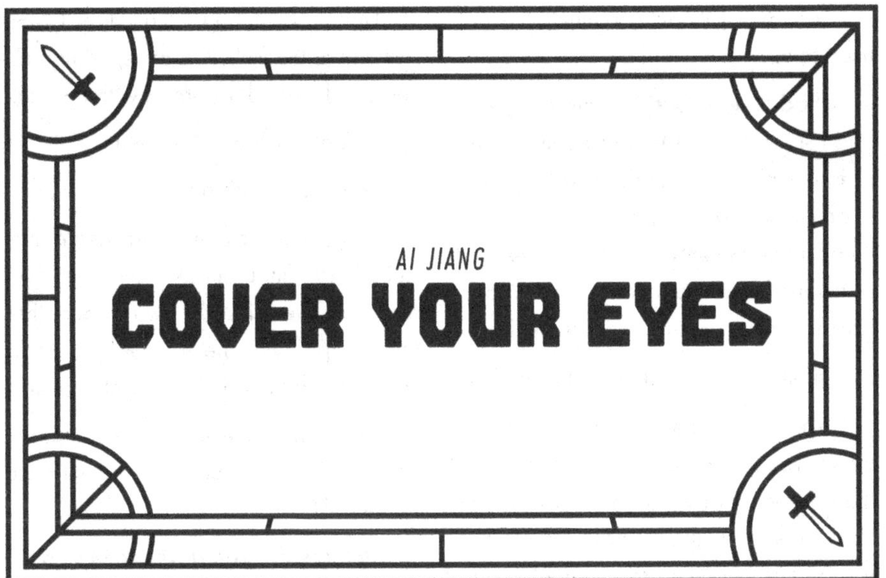

When I was six, I asked my mother, as she sat by my bed at noon, way past my bedtime, "Why don't we go out in daylight anymore?"

My mother laughed. "Why should we?"

She stroked my hair, urging me to sleep so she could slip away to the job that she was already late for.

Her response to me had been what her own mother told her when she was younger. I didn't question it before, and I still don't. The instilled fear of mornings was far greater than my curiosity. Until one day before her death, she told me, "Look outside when it's daylight."

But she never had the chance to tell me why.

I preferred sleeping with my back toward the window—as did everyone else—but not my mother. She always worked during daytime, when most of the world was asleep or waiting for nightfall, with alert minds and eyes pressed shut with effort. Day traffic was minimal but always sounded like screeching prey, or sometimes crawling predators. I kept my window closed and the curtain drawn—that was what my mother taught me.

But I never felt truly asleep when it was daytime. It always felt like the sun was watching me from outside the window. Maybe it was.

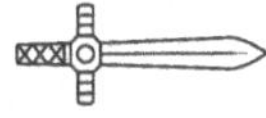

In the coffee shop, under fluorescent lights and an artificial glare, I told Kinqu about my insomnia.

"Don't worry about it so much. You get used to it."

It had already been twenty-five years, and I still was not used to sleeping in the presence of the sun during the day, though I had known no other routine. Next week I'll be turning twenty-six—the anniversary of my mother's death. It has been a decade, but it meant much more recently.

I shouldn't have looked out the window.

"When did *you* get used to it?" I watched mosquitoes crowd around the lightbulbs, thinking of the way most of us cower now from the sun. Unlike the past, insects that fed on flesh evolved to roam wherever was brightest, without fear.

A mosquito flew by Kinqu's head. He waved it away unconsciously and it flew towards me, landed on my arm. A prick. I let it be as it drank its fill, the way my mother would have let it. It amazed me still how fearless they were, showing such lust and greed in plain sight. The way they fed without consequence. They reminded me of the men in the photos that the police showed me when Mo—

"What are you doing tomorrow, during the day?"

I sniffed with minor annoyance. Kinqu knew what I would be doing during the day tomorrow, what most people also did.

I pressed my lips together, offering an unamused expression before I said, "Staying home."

He blew raspberries.

"Don't always be such a killjoy. Come with me to the club. Just once," Kinqu raised and lowered his brows with a smirk.

I shook my head. "Next time."

"You know that's a lie."

He crossed his arms. I watched a mosquito land. Kinqu smacked his hand over the insect, then flicked it away, not bothering to wipe away the leftover blood now smeared over a minuscule patch of skin.

From where we sat on the patio, we could see the TV screen near the entrance to the café.

"*Statistics. Everyone loves statistics, don't we?*" the news anchor woman asked her partner, a meek man who appeared to be a new addition to the segment.

"Y-Yes," the male anchor replied.

The anchor woman's smile seemed to twitch, though it remained taut. Her red lips always looked too bright. "*With everyone remaining indoors during the day—or at least most,*" she raised a brow, "*there has been a significant decrease in violence.*"

The anchor woman then jumped into those statistics, offering charts and diagrams I had no interest in. Kinqu's eyes were glued to the screen. Their reasoning made little sense to me, but I knew better than to question the government's logic. It seemed that more than enough people believed it anyhow... like Kinqu.

I pressed my lips into a thin line, thinking of my mother. They had said no one

would dare attack in plain sight, but still...
And it was never reported on the news.

"See? It's perfectly safe," Kinqu said, gesturing to the screen.

I shook my head. It wasn't, but there was no sense trying to argue with someone who wouldn't listen.

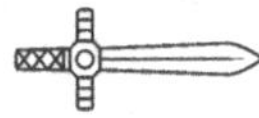

I watched the light bleed into the sky, starting from the end of the street. When night was halfway gone outside my window, I hung up my new curtains.

The tarpaulin fabric of this set smelled stale and was thicker and more opaque than the almost translucent cotton that I had before. But that set felt comforting—they had soaked up the smell of coffee and the clean-laundry air freshener that floated in my room. These new curtains offered a greater sense of safety in the darkness they provided.

It wasn't what Mother would've wanted, but what she'd said about not needing to be fearful was proven wrong the day she passed.

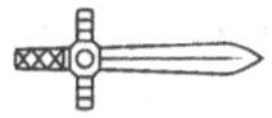

"I bought new curtains," I said to Kinqu when I settled down in front of him at the café the next night.

There were no mosquitoes today. The ice clinked and scraped against the inside of my glass, disturbing the iced latte before it stilled—muffled screeching.

"Still can't get used to it, huh?"

Kinqu glanced at me from the corner of his eye before refocusing on the waitress walking by. He'd been trying to get her attention for weeks after noticing the brooch she always wore on her uniform—one with the logo of a band he liked. I could never remember the name, but I caught snippets of the music once, and they were always shouting about seeing clearer in the dark.

Kinqu sported tight shorts, like always, while I sweltered in my sweats. My stomach boiled as Kinqu's gaze continued to follow the waitress. I popped an ice cube into my mouth. The mosquitoes returned.

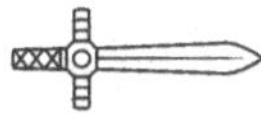

"Today. Come on, it's your birthday. Let's go to the club in the morning," said Kinqu, eyes twinkling with mischief.

I shook my head. I didn't know why he always bothered asking if he already knew what my answer would be, and where he conjured the constant hope that perhaps one day I'd change.

Shadows darted out across the street—people late for work. The bus's tail lights gleamed at the corner. A lost cause. No point trying to catch up now. I imagined Mother fast-walking in the daytime when the buses didn't run. Perhaps if they did—

"It's also my mother's anniversary. You already know we always celebrate with brunch at midnight."

Though Kinqu and I have been friends for years—an odd combination of extrovert and introvert—our often-conflicting thoughts could make it feel as though he were a stranger.

The comforting darkness wavered in the sky. My palms were clammy. I wiped them against my leggings, the fabric making me feel like a bound sausage.

Kinqu took a quick look at my outfit choice and his eyes twitched. Though he never voiced it, he wished I didn't feel the need to cover myself, to hide. But he understood my worries, and he knew what happened to Mother.

It wasn't her fault, he'd said.

No, it wasn't, but it was better to be safe—though I wished we didn't have to be so careful with our bodies because of the darkness gnawing at the minds of some. I looked down at my sweats—at least this was something I could control.

I waved away a mosquito.

"Next time, then," he said, but his attention had already moved elsewhere.

The waitress was nowhere to be found. Kinqu's eyes kept roaming the streets. I swiped the condensation from my glass and flicked it at his face. He turned with a scowl.

"Who are you looking for?" I asked.

He shook his head, eyes downcast. "No one." Kinqu chewed his upper lip. "It's not as scary as you think, you know."

He looked up at the moon, but he was referring to the sun. I wasn't sure if he was trying to convince me or himself, but his words held a hint of hesitance.

There was laughter in the distance coming from a group of men. They were looking in our direction. I stiffened. My eyes met with one of the men standing near the front of the pack.

"Early risers," I muttered, eyes flitting away. "I see them around sometimes, wandering the streets when I'm heading home a bit too late. Always got the crazed look in their eyes..." I refocused on Kinqu. "Do you ever see them... *do* anything?" I thought of the crime reports.

"Nope. I'm telling you. It's perfectly safe. Numbers don't lie!" Kinqu shook his head. "They've even cut down on the police force."

That worried me.

"Be careful, alright?"

Kinqu rolled his eyes but nodded.

I smacked the mosquito that landed on my arm; its crumpled wings glinted in the fairy lights the café hung up along the outdoor seating area. Smooth jazz played from the speakers, but I couldn't help imagining the saxophone's squeal coming from the dead insect smeared on my skin.

"It is."

In both our hands, Kinqu and I clutched the same coffees, munched on the same croissants for breakfast, and waited for the moon to shine at its brightest before we parted ways. We had been friends for years, but it always surprised me how similar, yet different, he and I were. Like my mother, Kinqu also worked during the day. I tried to convince him to take a night shift, but he refused. Kinqu's the only one I had left.

I left Kinqu with the dead mosquito. Mother was waiting.

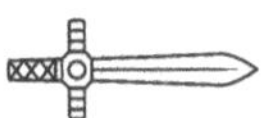

"It's getting warmer," I said when I sat down next to my mother's gravestone. I set an alarm for twenty minutes before 4 am, when the sun would rise. One hour would be enough. "The days are getting longer again."

I pulled at the grass and watched as the blades fell when I dropped them.

"I'll be starting at that café you used to work at—dawn? I asked for the night shifts, but I think they might give me a few day ones too... They're still open for twenty-four hours, except Sundays. You'd think they'd learn after you—"

I wasn't sure why I wanted to work the same job that caused my mother's death. The same position, the same hours—or what would be the same hours.

"It'll be okay though, right?"

Maybe I was hoping she'd rise from her grave, shake my shoulder, tell me not to do it.

"Right?"

My alarm went off, but the sun was early, a crescent peeking through trees that blocked its red and orange body. It was too early. I scrambled to my feet, kissed my mother's gravestone, and ran out of the cemetery onto the empty streets as the light chased me from behind.

I slowed to a walk halfway home, panting, lungs burning. The sky was pink, like washed-out flesh, and lightened by the second. When my breathing evened out, I heard footsteps behind me. My lips dried. I was still far enough from my house that quickening my steps would only draw more attention, signal alarm—danger.

I turned.

A man in his forties, dressed in a tweed coat with a matching hat, treaded behind me at a leisurely pace. He looked harmless enough, but my heart still pounded faster, trying to force its way from the confines of my ribs. I turned again to watch him as I walked. Then again. Again. Again. Again. Then—

He noticed.

I bit my tongue. He smiled apologetically and crossed the street, picked up his pace so he walked ahead of me rather than behind, even with the width of the road between us. I watched his back until he turned the corner.

I didn't breathe until I reached home. I didn't breathe as I struggled to open the front door. I didn't breathe when I dashed into the house, slammed the door behind me, collapsed onto all fours, heart and lungs dropping onto the carpeted floor. I finally breathed when I drew my curtains.

On my bed, I pulled the blankets around me, drenching myself in darkness.

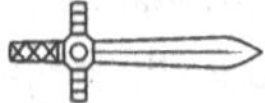

"Open. The. Window."

A scream. But my window remained closed, muffling the sound. The light had already crawled in, and with it, the muted noises of the day.

I was sixteen years old at the time.

I covered my ears, eyes squeezed shut, and remained immobile when the police arrived, immobile when they left. At the station, I didn't speak.

During the day, when they finally brought me home, I listened, watched, but I couldn't tell if it was the light that had burned my eyes or if it was the unseen events that had unfolded beneath my dreadful window. Why did Mother want me to open the window?

After two days of sleeplessness, exhaustion forced my eyes to flutter shut. I wondered what else I could possibly do but continue keeping my curtains open, the glass screen unlatched, pulled upwards.

After a year, I returned to the dark. That was what Mother would have wanted.

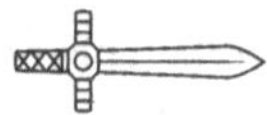

From behind the drawn curtains, my room looked still. Not a single shadow passed through navy drapes, black in the dark, though the ceiling seemed to swirl as my eyes adjusted to the lack of light.

I'd forgotten to close the windows.

A light, passing breeze pushed against the curtain. A sliver of light leaked through, casting jagged shadows across the walls. The ceiling continued to swirl with the light. Shadows mocked me with their gnarled limbs. A high-pitched scream drifted in through the window.

Mother?

I should close it. That was what they told us to do on the news, what they insisted we do. The scream weakened, faded. My heart hammered—ice against ice within my body.

They don't want us to see...

Mother?

They don't want us to care...

Because they, themselves, don't want to care...

With a sudden rush of adrenaline, I leapt from my bed and ripped the heavy drapes apart, allowing the bright noon sun to stream into the room.

Outside, below my window, in the middle of the road, was Kinqu, battered from what I could see. Bruises—brown and purple, like rotting fruit in the fridge—blossomed across his eyes, nose, elbows, and knees. He rose, dragging himself forward at an impossibly slow pace, knees trailing rust; a snail stuck in its own slime. Behind him loomed a man—the same one from before?

No. Different. Closer and closer, until he nipped at Kinqu's heels.

COVER YOUR EYES

Kinqu was missing one shoe, the other Converse frayed from the dragging. The man snaked a hand around Kinqu's waist, covering his eyes with the other. And it was as though covering Kinqu's eyes, shielding them from the light, caused him to suddenly lose consciousness. But what the man had caused was nothing but momentary blindness, the illusion of darkness—something we had been taught meant safety even in the most dangerous of situations.

There was a false sense of security, of ease, of a strange kindness in darkness, and of blindness.

I threw open my window, eyes squinting and spasming uncontrollably in the light. "Kinqu!"

Mother.

The man looked up, his mask too opaque and my vision too impaired for our eyes to meet. Kinqu squirmed, his head flailing, searching for the direction of my voice.

The pause lasted less than a few seconds before I tore out of my room, bare feet propelling me past Mother's empty bedroom, down the stairs, barely halting before I slammed into the front door. I took an umbrella from a stand by the door, the one Mother always brought with her to work. There was no time to find a proper weapon.

"Kinqu!"

Mother.

I rounded the house, screaming nonsensical words, hoping to draw attention, get others to open their curtains, or even come out of their house—a futile hope. The man was running down the street with Kinqu abandoned where I'd seen him last.

"Kinqu?"

Mother?

No response.

I tented the black umbrella and raised it above us, hiding us from the sun. Kinqu's chest rose and fell, arrhythmic and erratic.

"Help!" I called. "Help!"

But there was no sound, only the insistent buzzing of invisible mosquitoes in my ear. My eyes spun around, searching, looking at everything but seeing nothing. Mother's laughter echoed in my head.

So blind. So very, very blind.

"Fire!" The voice that ripped open my lips was a high-pitched wail, a raw croaking that gurgled in my throat. "Fire!"

And soon, windows stood with parted curtains, shadows lingering behind glass. The streets pooled, a river of blurred figures scuttling into the light, surrounding us in a crowd, mouthless whispers.

Fear not for us, not a young girl bawling in the streets or a young man on the verge of death, but for their own lives amid a false fear of a wild blaze trailing.

My shoulders relaxed, though my fingers remained tight claws curled around the handle of the umbrella. My eyelids fluttered, vision still unfocused, until something pulled me upwards.

"No," I said. "Kinqu." I pointed.

The umbrella fell from my hands, and I grabbed at it blindly.

"Where's the fire?" they asked, the question echoing, repeating, hands pulling at me, shaking me, pecking at me from all directions. "Where is the fire?"

I pointed to myself and the fractured-ness they could not see. Then I pointed at Kinqu, who now had his own hands covering his eyes, knees drawn over his naked chest. There was the sound of a phone beeping, someone dialing, hope-fully for help. The crowd began to disperse when the sirens wailed in the distance—until there was but a handful left.

A voice came from my left, toward the hand that still had hold of my elbow. "Can you walk? Can you see?"

I shook my head. *No. No. No.* There was movement, and the red behind my closed eyelids dimmed. I paused, then opened my crusting eyes in slow motion.

"Can you walk? Can you see?"

I looked up at the opaque skin of the black umbrella, then at the face of my res-cuer—an elderly woman who lived down the street—flanked by a young couple who had just moved into the neighborhood. A man, the same one who had crossed the street for my comfort earlier, crouched over Kinqu with a blanket.

"Yes," I nodded, my hand wrapping around the woman's, over the umbrella handle. "Yes."

It is safe, it is safe, if we just make it so.

Mother.

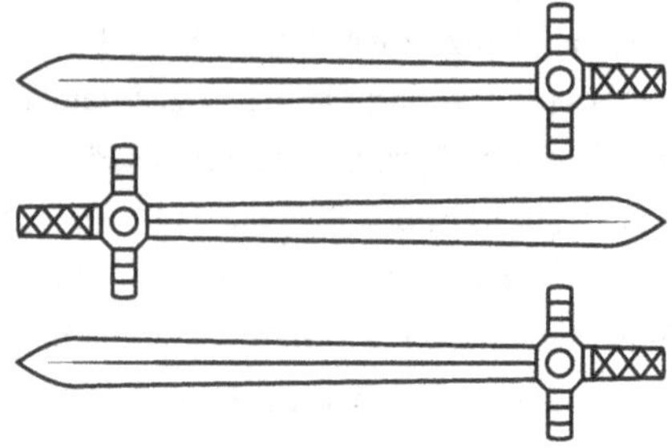

VI
OF CUPS

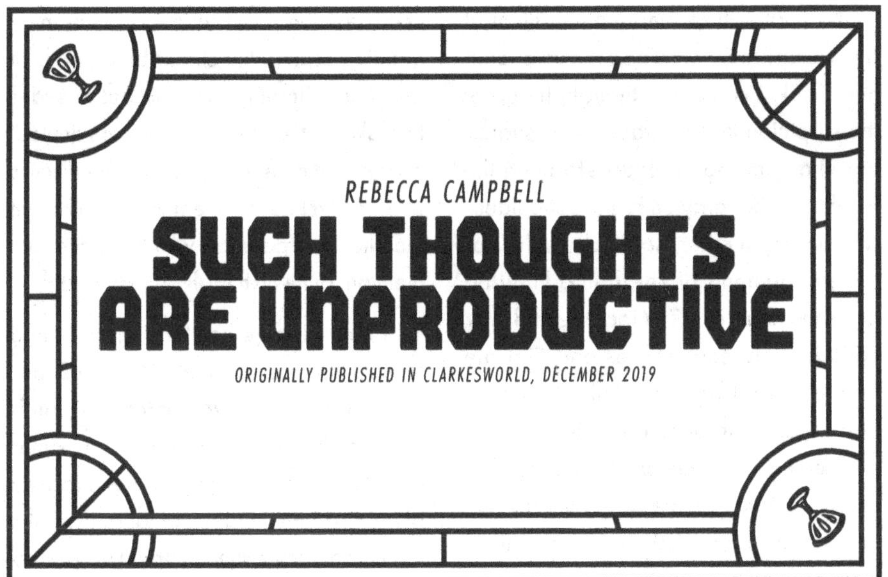

The woman whom I sometimes belie-ved to be my mother flickered. Once. Twice. Her face—smiling—froze in a cloud of pix-els, while her arm—the wide, emphatic gestures that were as much a marker of her identity as the color of her eyes or her fin-gerprints—swept the screen, leaving blue eddies, whirlpools of information. Then silence, but her mouth moved, leaving a flesh-colored smudge across the top half of her head.

"You've cut out again," I said. The pic-ture reset. She was saying something that made her laugh.

"Your hair looks really good," I said.

"Wha—"

I waited. Repeated myself.

"Yes," she said, suddenly clear, "I cut it myself because the guy they get in is terrible. He let me use his scissors, at least. So chic and DIY. If it was 2015 I'd pin it—"

Slideshow, for which I was paying five dollars a minute. Figures in black pacing against the yellow cinder block wall of the common room. I tried not to look at them because it was always better not to look at them. It was better when I could see the windows and get a look at where she was.

"We're running out of time," I said. "I only paid for fifteen minutes, cause last time you had the drill and I thought that maybe—"

The hand, now trailing pixels. It was definitely her face, but I searched her jaw-line for the suture where her appearance had been attached, virtually, to this body, a scrim of pixels over the person that was— as far as anything was these days—my mother. Her smile. Her expressive hands.

No matter how empty the content of our words, there was comfort in seeing her speak. I could not, though, let go of the suspicion that this face I was searching—hanging again, lag deforming the number on her gray uniformed shoulder—was not my mother, so much as the collected fragments of her from a hundred thousand hours of CCTV footage and intercepted video conferences and Google hangouts and whatever other material had streamed through the state's huge filter-feeding machines, snuffling all traffic—dark and light, private or public—for the information it required on problematic—

—Such thoughts are unproductive.

This woman that I speak to, who is my mother, and may not be my mother, but who fills the space in my life called mother. I will continue to chat with her when I can because the illusion—if it is an illusion—is so close to reality that sometimes I am taken in and relax into daughterly affection.

The black silhouettes in the background of the common room do nothing to interfere with our conversation because no part of our conversation can be hidden from the eye that watches us all, which is not an eye, but the hundred thousand eyes of a filter-feeding behemoth made entirely of information.

She sends me messages at night, long discourses on the problem of making the food palatable, or the solitaire she plays, or the Scrabble tournaments she organizes.

I can hear the powerful gears of her mind grinding against the cinder block walls of the place, finding things to put in order, to make, to fix. Her resources are limited: games and other companions, the discussions and lectures and regular chastisement that she undergoes, but which she does not mention, but which is always implied.

I can imagine her turning that mind toward the problem of 2 + 2 being 5, producing the right answer for the individuals who ask her—daily, hourly, by the minute—to repeat this new truth. A problem of philosophy? Perhaps of language, she would say, from the perspective of neo-radical-orthodoxy, or post-Platonism. One needs only to adjust the definitions in that portion of one's brain that is cordoned off from reality in order to comply with the ideologies of the state. That's how she could give the "right" answer without dying of it.

She never says these things.

The mother who exists in my mind—which might, or might not, align with the mother on the screen, or in my messages—would do such things. It would be necessary for her survival, once the small collection of paper books had been arranged by the Library of Congress system, with gaps on the shelf for "critical theory" and "resistance" and "escape plans."

But what kind of escape could she possibly need? The enclosures are beautiful, despite the yellow cinder block walls. I've seen them when her back is to the window, trees and mountains framed in

SUCH THOUGHTS ARE UNPRODUCTIVE

bulletproof glass. When I was a kid, we often drove through the Rockies and stopped at Banff. Once, we stayed in a massive château on Lake Louise. There were men and women in lederhosen outside, playing alphorns. The air, when we left the sticky lowland fug of our car, was so fresh and lovely I wanted to laugh. The glaciers had receded, but you could still see the blue-white glow of them up high, far beyond us.

I think—I'm not sure—but I think I have seen similar mountains in the brief moments when she directs the camera over her shoulder and out the window. The time zone can't be far too different, but the summer nights are bright there, so it must be farther north. Toad River, I think. One of the big provincial parks. I have looked at maps—antique ones on paper, tearing at the folds—and seen the gaps in the satellite images, and I have wondered, is she there? Close to 60?

This winter, I'll watch the angles of sunlight and track the darkness behind her. I'll hope she picks up on my questions: I've had trouble with my nasturtiums again. Are you growing anything? And hope she turns her camera toward the window, talks about what she's planted in the gardens that are supposed to be so therapeutic.

We live in an age of infinitely preserved information, so it's not actually odd that I saved every video call on an external hard drive. At night, I turned off the Wi-Fi and studied my mother's face for evidence of fakery. I didn't search for "ten ways to spot deepfakes" because that left fingerprints, and I'm already a problematic citizen, confirmed as such by my associations, rather than any action I have taken. To be visible meant you have done something to deserve visibility, after all. And if our exploration of the human genome means anything, it's that my genes matter. I am treacherous.

You could inherit treachery, or be infected with it, by the people who waited in government offices, slouching from hard blue chair to hard blue chair, sharing between them the rumors and possibilities regarding what happened to the missing. Camps. Education centers. Wilderness highways that stopped dead on the other side of the great divide. The blank spots that are slowly overtaking our digital maps, even archived versions I thought I had kept safe. No more news from Fort Mac, not for a couple of years now. The pipelines never leak. Silence accompanied any disruption of gasoline, or the regular oil slicks up and down the Salish Sea, where all the fish are dead. There's another dam on the Peace River to celebrate, but the blackouts got worse.

When I had thoroughly and silently examined the information available (is that a tamarack? A black spruce? Is that a mountain?) It occurred to me that as the woman I talk to might be scrimmed with my mother's face, so might be the room in which she sat. The darkness and light I have so painstakingly tracked, the faint, blue line of a mountain, and a pink winter sunset at three in the afternoon? That may well mean nothing. Worse than nothing: deception.

At work, I was also a watcher. I was part of a team that sanity-checked the AI that surveils traffic errors in the western provinces. I looked for anomalies and found ways to integrate them into the AI's understanding, slowly eliminating my own job, as the anomalies grew rarer and the world more perfectly known. I thought, sometimes, following on my father's philosophical leanings, that this was the goal of our state: perfect knowledge of landscapes and people and relationships. So perfect that the simulacrum we saw on the screen was more perfect than the territory we possessed. The woman on the screen was my mother, as was the woman in my messages, so perfectly had she been synthesized by the state that also slit—

—Unproductive.

"Have you heard from Da—"

"—He's okay. Did you get that? You're a slideshow."

"Weak—"

I was a slideshow, too. Maybe she didn't even think it was me. Maybe there was another woman that she spoke to midweek, and she believed that was the real daughter, and she only spoke to me because the system required her to maintain the fiction. Maybe she had a million daughters asking her leading questions.

Maybe.

Still smiling, in case we connected, I wrote on my tablet and held it up to my phone: HE'S STILL WORKING ON THE SOLAR PANELS.

Dad withdrew from the city to our old cabin in the interior (is she near there? Farther north and east. The forests I have seen out that window are deep and green), when Mom left, or disappeared, or was taken, whichever mode you choose to use for description. Dad and I just say "when Mom left" like it's the only date that matters. He hasn't come back to the city since. I took two weeks off from work to help him chuck their things, and carry what was important—photographs, old books, her clothes, her jewelry—to the cabin. We couldn't afford to take much, with the cost of gas. The house was requisitioned later, for a nominal fee that didn't cover the time or gas it would have taken him to get the papers signed. I don't go by there anymore. I don't like to see it.

"Do you remember when we camped at Banff?"

"When you graduated from high school? Or are you talking about before Sophie's wedding?"

"Sophie? Piano teacher? At Banff?"

"Aunt Sophie, not piano Sophie. We were roommates all through grad school. If you were going to have a godmother, she would have been your godmother. You were pretty little that trip, though."

I remember Banff, because we went right up to the glacier and Dad showed me

SUCH THOUGHTS ARE UNPRODUCTIVE

where it had been each year, walking backward through time, saying this is when you were born and this is when I was born.

"I was like five? Four? I thought that was Emily's wedding."

"No, Sophie. And I was maid of honor so I had to be there three days early, and you and Daddy just ate junk food and went on the swings until you threw up. You hated Fudgsicles for a year after that summer. I should have done that with more junk food. You'd be vegan now."

I actually *am* vegan. I do not remember having an aunt named Sophie. I'm pretty sure it was Emily's wedding.

Dad and I played on the merry-go-round until we were so dizzy, we stumbled across the soccer field toward the edge of the forest, collapsing on the grass until the world stopped spinning and we'd expelled all the Doritos and gummy worms we'd eaten. That afternoon, Mom—woozy and white-faced after a late night—got ready in a blue dress I had never seen before, her hair up high and her makeup all pretty.

She carried me into this old lodge halfway up the mountain and shouted over my shoulder to friends I had seen in pictures, but never met, making jokes about things I didn't understand. Dad and I left during the dancing, but she came in long after that, laughing. She slept in late, grouchy, cuddling a water bottle to her pillow, while we went driving in search of coffee and hot chocolate.

"And what do you say to more Doritos, Mar?" Dad asked, and I pretended to throw up.

She said other things that left me watchful and adrenalized. I didn't draw attention to the discrepancies because her memory might be flawed, but so was mine. So was everyone's, except for the filter-feeding behemoth that follows us all, and while we didn't seem to possess the same past, it possessed us equally.

We found an equilibrium. For more than a year I didn't even hear from her, not even to confirm she still existed. I waited patiently in offices, both virtual queues and in person, and I went to Victoria to line up with all the others at the Ministry of Information Management and Retrieval. The answers were always the same: here's a chit with a number. We'll be in touch. Said with a synthetic smile by an AI phone tree, or a tired clerk behind glass. They will always get back to you.

I am patient and consistent, also better connected than a lot of people, so I have pushed further than most. I also know the system better, and know when to leave things be, keep my head down, be grateful that I know my mother is alive. I am the model supplicant, waiting in dove-like patience outside the walls for the emergence of her mother, whose radical spirit has been (will be) corrected by the benevolent ministrations of the state.

You got to know other people because you saw them at the offices and in the spillover corridors. Which wasn't to say you knew them, just that you were familiar with their faces and concerns. Julie's looking for her brother and nephews. Chris wants to find his wife—he thinks she's in the foothills somewhere. Alberta has a few sites.

You avoided the ones with loud voices who talked too loud about what was happening, even the explanations you really shouldn't say out loud: they have been replaced by bots of some description; their minds are being damaged beyond coherence by electroshock or DBS. Uncommon, but appealing: discrepancies are coded messages that only family will recognize, and thus communicate important information about location, and security movements, and the details of what is happening inside, in preparation for a massive action. We should all pool the discrepancies, and see what picture they show us, if we stand far enough back. We should talk. We should organize.

I've never contributed to these efforts. In lineups—the sorts of lineups that involve standing up every fifteen minutes to move one spot down in the long row of hard blue chairs—I listened, but said nothing, only thought, you don't know how loud your voice is why don't you care that the walls are full of cameras and your face is so well known to the machine no one you love can ever be sure that it's you talking to them.

I didn't need specifics regarding what happened inside, because what happened inside is what's happened inside such

education centers since they were first invented. Repetition and regulation. Rote recitation of truths regarding the nature of the society to which we belong. The principle being—I knew this, because Mom told me—that the surface recitation has a transformative effect on the mind, even if the mind resists the meaning of the words it says.

And then the culturally-specific humiliation, and the strategic application of pain—

"—Recite platitudes that deny climate change," she said, "or the refugee crisis or ethnic cleansing or forced sterilization or eugenics. The perfectibility of the human animal in an ideal society. Repeat it and eventually you believe it. Or act like you believe it, which is just as good as far as they're concerned."

That was near the end, when she said those sorts of things out loud, and in text, and every last fragment collected and shared them across whatever the network is now. Five Eyes. Nine Eyes. Ten Billion Eyes. In collaboration, those systems extracted meaning and implication from the marks she made on the screens and the sounds from her mouth—rarely out of range of a microphone—cross-referencing those patterns with other patterns. They flagged her profile. They saw the outcomes, and they identified my mother as a point of vulnerability.

In her terms: an imperfect citizen.

Me too, probably, and Dad, though we are less threatening. We don't talk often anymore. It was difficult to have a

     SUCH THOUGHTS ARE UNPRODUCTIVE

conversation when most of what matters is dangerous to say out loud. Dad mentions that he's repainting the garage. I talk about how I want to do a bike trip through Oregon. Dad says he thinks he's got a rat in the basement. I say that I had some decent wontons at a new place that opened around the corner.

Hanging over our conversation, a list of things we don't mention: droughts (unless historical); disappearing island chains; climate refugees; the rage associated with rising temperatures and food prices; the—

—But this isn't productive.

We both know. We talk about whether he can catch the rat with a humane trap. We talk about how smart rats are, and how deftly they have adapted to human landscapes. I say I'll make a trip to help. He says no no, no need. I'm fine. I say, you should come visit me, do city stuff, and he says no no no, no need. I'm fine. We're both fine. As you can see, I am now good at lying.

I ran into an aunt at some event, and she said, "I haven't heard from your mom in ages, how is she?"

"Oh. She's doing better."

"Better? What happened?"

"She contracted one of the antibiotic-resistant strains of TB, and she's taking some time to recover."

"I'm so sorry to hear it. Where is she?"

"One of the new sanatoriums. She'll be in for a while."

"Oh, Mar. She'll be in my thoughts. Pass that on, would you? Or maybe I'll email her."

This was the safe response. An innocuous message passed on. No further inquiry. No possibility of betrayal.

I set my keys on the little shelf by the door and sighed, the way you do when you take off high heels or get somewhere quiet where you can cry. Then I heard someone shifting on my couch.

She squealed. "Mar! Mar! Look at you! The last time I saw you was at your mom's fiftieth. When was that? Oh god don't tell me. That means we're old."

I have an Aunt Sophie. She was a thin, athletic woman, honey-brown hair, not Mom's pixie cut, but of the same vintage, choppy, with playful silver highlights. She was dressed in elegant athleisure. And you know, at that moment she could have been an aunt—one of the women from Mom's PhD program, or a second cousin, or someone from the Elder college where she talked political philosophy.

"Where did you—?"

"—I'm just going to be in town for a couple of weeks, and I'll be nearby while I deal with a contract. I saw your mom, you know."

"What?"

"Last week. That's why I'm here. I knew you were in the city, but I didn't know where, obviously, and—okay, I was a little embarrassed that I've been so out of touch with everyone. It's these short contracts. They're disorienting. I travel. So. Much."

"You heard from Mom?"

"Yes. And I realized how much of your life I've missed these last years. Remember when I lived on Elm Street and you guys used to come over and we'd go to that one park with the splash pad, and then we'd get ice cream on the drive?"

I found myself nodding. It's what you do. Lie.

"Anyway," my new aunt said, "I thought I'd come over and I had your mom's key so. I brought you dinner, too. Are you still vegan?"

"Yes," I said. "For five years now."

"Good. You know, while I was waiting I remembered how much you hated cooking when you were a teenager—remember how your mom tried to teach you to make, I don't know, spaghetti sauce, and the fights. Oh God. I heard about the fights."

I had not remembered those fights in years. "The Bolognese," I said. "I still can't make it. On principle."

"I brought pakoras. They're off the fucking hook—I ate like two of them waiting for you. Let's go eat the rest."

The pakoras were excellent. The rice she also brought was fragrant and nutty underneath the curry. The beer delicious, bubbling out of our glasses and over the rough table on my back deck, which just had room for four people. Sophie talked about grad school and Mom, about the parties they threw together, about staying up late crying over deadlines and

supervisors, about graduation, and how Mom had blown hers off for the government job, but been there the next year for Sophie's, already pregnant with me.

"So you were at my graduation. Good luck charm."

I slid into this the way we slid into so many things: the loss of cities to the encroaching waters and deserts, the swamps and the Zika virus creeping north along the Mississippi, as the days grew hotter and the mosquitoes adapted. A kind of compliant quiet—pleasant, safe—overtook me as I thought yes, of course I had an aunt named Sophie. Of course.

She slept that night on the couch. It was the obvious thing to do. Curfew.

That night, I lay in my bed and recited the facts of my life: I do not have an aunt named Sophie; my mother did not have antibiotic-resistant TB and was not in a sanatorium on one of the quarantine islands. My mother is in an internment camp with yellow cinder block walls, somewhere in the mountains, far enough north that she's surrounded by tamarack, maybe by black spruce. At the end of the road with no exit. Britney is gone. The dam on the Peace River was bombed last year. Gasoline shortages are worse.

In the dark, I texted Mom, or the Mom-function of some bot, or the person who is assigned to be my mom that shift while my real mom—the internal enemy—underwent her daily reeducation, which wasn't happening but was happening all the time.

     SUCH THOUGHTS ARE UNPRODUCTIVE

Maybe, I thought, as I typed, these words are shuttling right out to the living room, where my Aunt Sophie was not sleeping, but surveilling the various fictions of my family relationships. I wondered how many nieces and nephews she had.

» *Sophie is here.*

« *Who?*

The answer came too quickly. Maybe she wasn't sleeping. She had trouble sleeping, she said, despite all the fresh air and exercise. Maybe she wasn't Mom, maybe she was—

» *Sophie. My aunt.*

« *Awesome. How is she? I haven't seen her for ages. She asked about you, though. Not surprised she turned up. She just finished that contract in Halifax.*

» *She's great. She brought pakoras from the place on Main.*

« *Oh man. I miss those.*

» *They're really good. We have leftovers. I wish we could send them.*

« *I want pot stickers from Hon's. And honeymoon rice. Then we should go for gelato.*

» *Triple scoop, then back for another three.*

« *You should ask your dad if he'll come into town and have gelato with you.*

» *He's so busy.*

I didn't write he hates the city now or he hates people now or neither of us can afford the gas if we want to eat. I wrote,

he's so busy and somewhere, the mom-function, or the behemoth, took note.

« *Have you heard from Britney?*

And then I had to stop, because the question hurt so much, it didn't matter whether the woman on the other side was my mother, or a fiction, or some synthesis of true and false too complicated to understand.

You ask yourself as you read my record: why is she so compliant? Why doesn't she tell the woman who keeps visiting daily, bringing food and asking questions about work and dating and Mom and Dad, why doesn't she just say, you aren't my aunt, I don't have an aunt.

I answer: because this is what we all do. Because I don't want to end up removed to a complex somewhere in the northern mountains, where if I escaped the hundreds of km between me and a highway would kill me before any of the guards had to. Because things can always get worse for everyone involved. Because they need someone on the outside.

But also. Also. Because she knows that I love honeymoon rice, and that I would like nothing better than to gorge on pakoras and gelato with Mom and Dad, and talk about inconsequential things, without reference to—or—or—but rather what we watched on TV and whether it was a Mac's convenience or a 7-11 that we used to stop at on our way out of town for holiday road trips (it was definitely a 7-11). Whether the aphids are back on the nasturtiums. I talk this way with the entity who is/isn't my mother, who may be my mother, who may be human. The entity behaves so exactly like my mother, and I like that, because then I don't think about how she's dead, or in solitary, somewhere, with the volume on prog rock or economic propaganda at 79 decibels for weeks on—

—But this is not productive.

My face betrays itself to the camera that is watching me, that also hears the catch in my voice when I thank the barista for my coffee. I use the drive-through because it offers marginally more privacy, since it can't read your whole body, and because if you order with the app, the drink is there and you don't have to say anything and you have the pleasure of silence, though your face—the breathing, roughened by repressed tears—is still visible to it.

The girl who gives me her drink is impassive, but I think—a flicker of sympathy in her eyes? She can't tell that I'm contaminated by my association with my mother, that I have an Aunt Sophie. But maybe she's contaminated, too, and has an Aunt Sophie. Who knows? You don't wait long enough to find out.

Sophie and I watch movies and go for walks, and sometimes I think how much I would like it if Sophie was my aunt. She clucks over me when I cough and asks whether I've tried turmeric and makes me tea of mint and ginger. It would be very easy to accept the gentleness of this state-sponsored intervention, ignoring the deviations I hear in conversation, and the fact that she is also someone else's aunt. I like Sophie. That's what I keep thinking. I like her. It's such a relief to have someone like a mom around that I cry, sometimes, when she checks in to see if I ate lunch.

We walk past my neighbors who say, *who's that, Mar?* And I say, *this is my Aunt Sophie*, and they all smile, and I don't know—not really—if they believe me, or if Aunt has become code for them as it has for me, for something you can't talk about, a person who is close to you like a missing lover, like family, but who is—

Dad called. Unusual, therefore treacherous. "It's confirmed," he said.

Sophie was on the porch. She'd waved *yes yes* when I got the call, *take it*, and she kept eating. I'd made us cold noodles with mint and basil from the pot I kept in the corner of the little deck.

"When?"

"This morning. I'm going to head out tomorrow morning."

"I could be there—"

"—No, you can't. It's contagious. You'll have to get checked out. They'll be in touch. Probably soon."

"What do you need?"

"Nothing. Just to hear your voice."

In the silence my throat shut and on the other side of the line, his throat shut too. I tried to think of safe things I could say, but what would that even be? All conversations are recorded. All expression is evidence.

"What is it?"

"TB." He paused. "You know the one."

We all knew what that meant. There's nothing for us to say, because probably all the feelings, all the fear and anger, were exhausted that first year when we didn't hear from Mom, and he went with me to the offices with the hard blue chairs. Now, though, it was just the familiar and inexorable creep of the end, as all us imperfect citizens were taken up, one by one.

Sophie started as soon as I hung up the phone, "What happened?"

I said nothing.

"Talk to me, honey." Mom used to call me honey. She still did sometimes, in text. Sometimes she didn't.

"It's your dad, isn't it? I know how hard this is."

I threw things into my pack. T-Shirts. Socks. Solar charger. Filter bottle. Fleece.

"You can't go silent on me. Mar. Mar. Do you think that this is what your mother wants? Seriously? You have to talk."

Documents, hidden from her view by the closed door, on which she banged her fists, tucked into my waistband.

"It's not good to bottle everything up inside. You need to learn to trust people."

My backpack—the giant framed one Dad got for me to use on my first real solo expedition the summer I was twenty. It cost twice what I wanted, but he insisted, and he'd been right because here it still was. I checked my balance with Humanitas, the telecom provider for all of the camps. Sanatoriums. Whatever. Ten minutes banked against next week's call, and enough for a handful of texts, so I hit dial.

She didn't answer.

I rang again, just swallowing the five dollars. Then the woman appeared, her back to the windows.

"Hey, I didn't expect—"

The image of my mother-not-mother hung, and reflexively I studied the margins of her face for the suture between reality and fiction, the faint betraying lines of an AI's interference.

"You cut out."

"I didn't expect to hear from you. I heard from your dad yesterday, though, so both of you are off schedule. What's up?"

"Dad's sick."

The image hung. I picked up the jiffy I had ready in case, and began writing on the white wall of my bedroom: DAD IS SICK I'M GOING TO VISIT HIM.

Her face—hanging in the moment as she understood what I wrote—was animated only by the shimmer of pixels across my screen. She might have dropped, but I kept my phone fixed on the wall so she had a chance to see it again. One way or another, they already knew, and if it was Mom. If it was. *If.* Then she had to know.

"Are you talking to her? Is that her?" Sophie shouted. "You can't disturb her recovery, Mar. That's just fucking selfish."

She said other things in quick succession—about my being a bad daughter, about how I was a bitch, and about how I shouldn't be so hard on myself—careening from insult to affection in a split second in order to stop me from doing—something. I wondered if she'd try to hit me.

I locked up the apartment with Sophie still following me, talking about opening up, saying *are you a fucking rock? Tell me what's wrong with Bastien, he's my friend too, you can't shut me out.* A thousand other platitudes about sharing the burden of pain.

I got into the car. She stood in front of it.

"Why don't you just put a tracker on me," I said, "and let me go. It'll all be over soon anyway."

"I don't know what you're talking about."

I inched forward. She leaned onto the hood and I thought, this may be the single stupidest moment of my entire life.

"We're family, Mar."

Maybe she told the truth, though not in the way she thought. We were family in the sense that we were bound to the same omnivorous machine.

"Please," she said. "Please."

I could hear her saying those words to someone else, someone standing behind me, someone looking out of my eyes, and I wanted to ask, who is it? Who are you talking to?

I unlocked the door. She got in, face full of rage-tears.

"You can't rescue him," she said. "You need to just trust that things happen for a reason."

I thought about killing her. I thought about killing myself. I thought about driving into the roadblock at the exit for Needle Park, which was now manned by American uniforms, hazmat suits, trucks with Chinese plates.

But while I often have those thoughts, I have never pursued them. It's how I have survived as long as I have, why I haven't been scooped with my parents, with Brit—

—But thinking of Britney would make things even worse than they were. So instead, I thought about the roadblocks, and how the exits for Kingsvale and Brookmere and Coldwater were bulldozed, so you couldn't leave the car to feel the air change as you climb into the mountains. I thought about what might now be on the other side of the torn up concrete and rock.

She talked. She laughed. She told the same stories about my mother in grad school, what a mess she was during her comps, cleaning the bathroom at midnight, smoking until dawn on their tiny, rotten front porch. Ha ha ha.

I thought of all the times we started our summer road trips on the Coquihalla, headed to the cabin, or farther north and east. Other years, due south along the American coast, watching the beaches change from shingle to sand, to Manzanita and Tillamook, then farther south until we found our way to California. I thought of camping, and the dogs with me in the back seat.

Her throat raw with talk, she kept going, "Your parents love you so much," she said, "they want what's best for you, and what's best is to let them get better."

"We're going to need gas," I said. "Stop at Merritt."

"Are you even listening? I'm here because I love you, Mar, and because I'm trying to convince you to move on with your life, and let them go. You can't change this."

Once, a year ago, when I still hadn't heard from Mom, and Dad had just moved to the interior but was off the grid because of the fires, and the Coquihalla was still roadblocked because of the attack on the dam, and I had no idea about anything anymore, and Britney was—

—I had the opportunity to find an aunt, or a niece, or a cousin. This happened when you appeared to be as compliant as I did. Ashley—my direct manager—called me into a meeting with someone I'd never seen before, a woman in a sleek gray suit who talked about how I could help Britney and my mother and anyone else I cared to help, by telling them about my extended family, about those cousins I met sometimes on the hard blue chairs. I told them I didn't have any cousins like that, but that

I'd think about it. I wondered, later, if my hesitation was enough. Maybe we were all damned because I thought, instead of saying, *yes yes whatever you like, I'll find a cousin and tell you anything you need to know.*

The lineup at the gas station was better than Vancouver. Thirty minutes. I thought of killing her again, my Aunt Sophie, who had grown so familiar to me, messenger from a childhood I had not had, a life I did not lead in a country that no longer existed, full of loving familiar bonds, and gentle teasing, and a father not slowly dying of TB, a mother not being tortured by—

—I said, "There has to be someone that you're protecting, right?"

"You, Mar. You're my goddaughter," she said it mechanically, and I could imagine the dialogue somewhere in the dossier that archived me, identified my vulnerabilities, cataloged my failures. I have no godmother, no aunt, no mother, no wife. "I swore at your christening that I would uphold the ethical and social bond of our relationship. That I would love you. I promised—"

—We moved a car length forward. You could smell the wildfires, and see last year's burnout, overgrown with fireweed.

"Daughter?" I asked. "Your sister? A granddaughter?"

It was like a moonscape out there, Dad had said when he drove through after the fires. On the other side of the mountain, the cabin was safe, but probably not for many more seasons. I had always thought that I could escape there, if I needed to, get the camping gear and walk out to some place no one will ever set foot. A mountain. A valley where I could wait until this was over.

"You should probably go see them," I said. "Whoever they are. They'd rather see you than get whatever help you think they'll get. Because you're not helping. Not really."

When we got to the pump, I filled up then we went inside to pay, and get some water, and whatever candy was available because that's what you do in Merritt, you get snacks for the last two hours on the road, even if they were sparse and over-priced gummy worms.

She said, "You know I don't have a choice."

I nodded.

"She's not your mother, probably—the one you talk to. You know where your mother is. You know what they do."

I nodded.

"I did actually know your parents in grad school. I did. You were in utero at my graduation. That's why they thought—and I was already doing. It. This. For her. I was doing it because if I don't—"

—And I will grant her a little privacy here. It only takes a few words when it's people like us, the imperfect citizens of this perfectly known world. She told me things that I do not wish to know, because they hurt to know, then we both looked instinctively for cameras and drones and microphones.

She said, "I have to. I'll just be. I have—" and she walked away.

I went back to the car and drank from the water bottle, then started the engine. A full tank of gas, the sunlight brilliant, and I pulled out of the lot. I had, I figured, a couple of hours before they got to me, and by then, I would be at Dad's, and maybe we could talk for a few minutes before they came.

I saw the signs for Peachland and Kelowna, and the sun was going down, and eating the gummy worms. I could almost be on one of those other road trips, out from the city to the cabin for a week, or maybe out past the mountains and somewhere else, north maybe. This time, I'd make Britney come with us, even if I had to beg her to take time away from work.

And—the image came to me, though I did not want it—Sophie with us, sitting up late to talk with Mom. I could imagine another lifetime in which she was my aunt, when she and her daughter might have joined us for a week on the lake, drinking beer by the water, and swatting at the mosquitoes together.

    SUCH THOUGHTS ARE UNPRODUCTIVE

II
OF CUPS

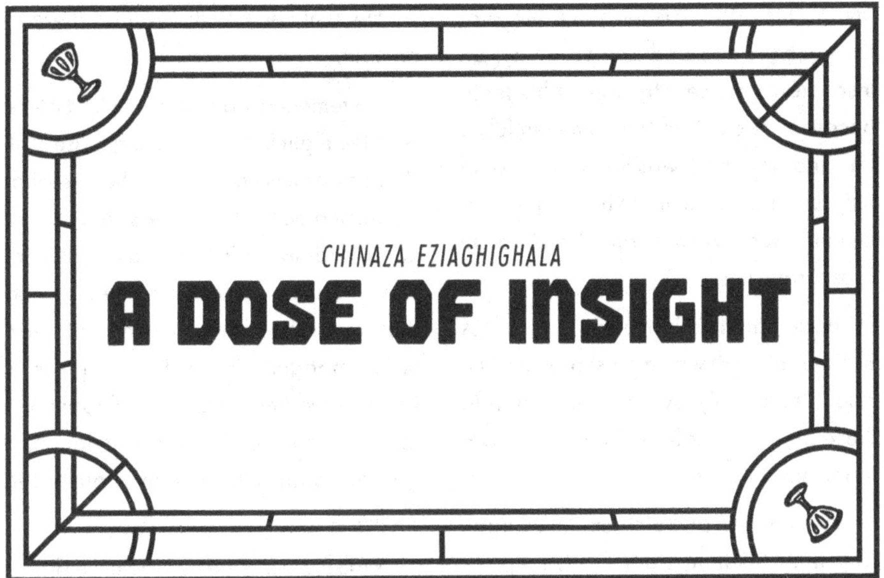

Bode felt everything.

He could feel his legs shattered in different places. He could not move his hands, but could feel that they were there. His breathing felt like that of a drowning man—suffocating. He felt a searing pain that started within his legs and ascended into his brain. There was a moistness in his trousers that felt like urine mixed with feces. He opened his mouth to scream, but it stayed shut—he could taste metal on his tongue. He willed himself to move, yet his body resisted. He could hear muffled screams as people gathered around his body.

They are standing too close, he thought.

He opened his eyes to see a man, dressed in briefs and a plain shirt, speaking into a phone with a hand on his blood-stained forehead. He tried to speak to the man, but his senses dulled. His eyes opened and closed, each closing drawing him deeper and deeper into unconsciousness. The last thing he thought about was Esosa's smiling face.

The last thing Bode heard was the sound of junior doctors' footsteps hurrying out of the call room, holding their noses—one stifling a giggle while avoiding eye contact.

Bode sat on the bed, pressing his thighs together in a tight clasp, watching people gather at the Accident and Emergency car park from his call room window: an old man gasping mouthfuls of breath, in obvious respiratory distress, an old woman thrashing her hands about while crying beside a dazed young man, resting his jaw on his palm. His eyes met those of the young man's and looked away, an insouciant glance. He sucked his teeth, because the call had been uneventful so far, and now here was work that would only further delay him. He had hoped that he could score a home run all the way to Esosa, now this.

Bode hated calls. He could care less. Besides, his shift was almost over and he had intentionally avoided attending to these people in order to hand them over to the morning team.

He glanced at the clock, and began to gather his things into his backpack, eager to leave before the end of his call time. From the entrance to the call room, Nurse Titi motioned for him to attend to the patient outside.

"Dr. Bode, emergency," she said, hands akimbo in the corridor. She then walked back to the triage area.

From the window, he watched as she walked to the people he had seen earlier. When he was sure that she was fully engaged, he grabbed his backpack and made his way to the back exit, to avoid the triage area and Titi's glare.

As he made his way to the back exit, he put his hands in his pockets, not hearing the anticipated jangle of car keys. Bode turned back to the call room in search of them. He found them nestled in the crevices of his call room mattress and grabbed them as a notification popped up on his phone; five missed calls from Esosa.

He sent her a text: *I will be there in an hour.*

He remembered how Esosa had come over the night before, wearing those pink shorts that he liked so much: the ones that contrasted against her dark skin. She had come to deliver his food, sashaying her way into the call room despite knowing that family members were not allowed there, engaging Titi with her dull jokes as Titi escorted her out of the call room. He could have sworn he heard Titi laugh, a foreign sound that remained etched in his mind.

Walking out of the call room, he dialed the colleague who was to take over for him. If he had looked through the call room window, he would have noticed that she was no longer outside.

Titi knew that the patient needed to be stabilized as soon as possible. This was why she went to get the oxygen tank herself instead of sending an attendant. Her stocky form pushed the cylinder in its trolly as she walked down the corridor, feigning fake smiles at passersby who greeted her.

She had notified Dr. Bode, as he was on call, even though she knew he could be indolent. He was short-tempered when overworked and even when the workload was lighter, he remained distant, his face in a ceaseless scowl that frightened everyone

     A DOSE OF INSIGHT

except her. The patient's wife said that he was suffering from chronic kidney disease and had not been dialysed for a month, because they could not afford it.

When she assessed him, he was barely conscious, but for his labored breathing. She knew admitting him would be futile because there was no bed space; she herself had sold the last one, which was in a private ward, to one of the hospital's affluent customers who had heart failure.

"Can you pay for bed space?" Titi asked. The patient's wife looked at her and gulped.

"How much?" the wife said.

"One hundred and fifty thousand naira."

"We don't have that kind of money," the wife said, raising her hands over her head.

So, Titi went to the oxygen room behind the Accident and Emergency department to get oxygen to stabilize him outside. On her way back to the car park, she intercepted Dr. Bode carrying his backpack.

"Nurse Tay Tayyy... no vex."

Nurse Titi said nothing, hissing and walking away, not expecting any less from him. This was why she preferred working with Dr. Frances instead; she was much nicer and had less air in her head. Bode, realizing the mess he must be in, bowed his head sheepishly and followed, like a young boy caught stealing money from his mother's purse.

At the car park, the old man was limp in the passenger's seat, his head resting on his chest, flanked by the old woman and young man Bode saw from the call room window.

"Doctor! My husband!" the old woman said between breaths, adjusting her wrapper around her waist. "He stopped talking... he was talking..."

"Madam, calm down."

Dragging his feet, Bode walked over to the man, took out his pulse oximeter, placed it onto his cold right thumb, and waited. There was no pulse. He used his stethoscope to listen to his chest. Nothing.

"Madam, he is dead," Bode said. "Why are we wasting time here?"

"I went to collect oxygen," Titi said. "Let's try to resuscitate."

Bode, ignoring her, took the documentation paperwork and wrote down: BID—"brought in dead"—then handed her back the form. Hiding her disgust, she made her way back to the Accident and Emergency entrance.

The old woman looked at him as if he had just spoken some strange language. She opened her mouth to speak, but no sounds came at first, then tears followed. The young man looked stunned—he opened the car door and sat in the back seat. Bode glimpsed his wristwatch and sighed, relieved he could get back to Esosa on time, and began walking away when a strong arm pulled him back.

"What do you mean by that? He was alive. We brought him in alive," the young man said, holding him by the collar. "We have been waiting while you were wasting time inside. I saw you, bastard!"

"If you touch me again, I will woze you," Bode said, pulling himself away from the young man as he raised his fists to his face and assumed a fighting stance. A trickle of doctors and nurses from inside the Accident and Emergency room watched from the windows.

"It will not be well with you."

Bode followed the voice to the old woman. Her eyes had darkened and lips were drawn in a scowl.

"Ko ni dafun e," she said. She began beating her chest in rhythm with her voice, repeating the same again and again in a murderous chant: "*It will not be well with you. Ko ni dafun e.*"

"Fuck off," Bode said, backing away and feeling for keys in his pocket. He stumbled across the door of his Corolla, got in and drove, watching from his rear-view mirror as Nurse Titi returned to the patient with a bag and mask.

Bode cursed Google under his breath. He had followed the map against his better judgment and the map had been wrong in its estimation—the traffic from Lagos Island was worse on this route. He had left his car on for the air conditioner, but it barely diffused the thick heat.

Esosa had called repeatedly to check on him because he was running late.

Tonight was their anniversary, and in typical Esosa fashion, she was planning the whole thing. They were to go to a fancy restaurant at Ikeja, and she'd arrived at the venue in the morning. He told her he would be late and she had been understanding. During the call, he had savored the memory of the first bite of her food and remembered why he had married Esosa in the first place.

She was just twenty years old—in her fourth year of medical school, while he was in his final year—when he asked her to go out to Freedom Park with him. He felt embarrassed about taking her there, but it was the only venue he could afford with its five-hundred-naira gate fee, and after hearing about her breakup he decided to seize his moment.

Sitting on a bench under the moonlit sky, they had talked about their plans for life after medical school; they were both going to the United Kingdom where he would be a respiratory physician, and she would be a dermatologist. When she had offered him the food in a flask, because "the food in Freedom Park was not worth all the money they would spend," he knew she was the one. They were married now, still in Nigeria almost five years after that meeting.

The map indicated that he was an hour away but, looking out the car window and seeing the multiple brake lights, Bode was not so confident. When the person in front of him moved forward, he saw the diversion that led to the other side of the road, where an adjacent street could easily connect him to the restaurant. He veered, turning off his headlights, but leaving his hazard lights on in hopes that oncoming cars could see him.

His mind went back to the old woman from earlier, and he suppressed a shiver that coursed through his body. He had never been one to fear people, but the woman had a certain unnerving quality about her.

A body panic hit him. As he struggled to breathe, feeling his hands becoming cold and clammy on the steering wheel, his eyes widened, and he saw large looming headlights as a truck swerved across his path.

Bode was seated in the car's passenger seat, flanked by a familiar old woman and young man. He looked down at hands that did not belong to him; then he looked at the side mirror to see a reflection of the old man, eyes staring back at him, mouth wide open as he touched his face—the reflection of the old man did the same in tandem.

He saw a flash of the old man's memories: a gathering of people, clad in black robes, kneeling around a red altar. Among these people were the old woman and a well-built man dressed in crimson robes. The man walked to him, sprinkling white powder around him, forming a white circle of dust on the red altar.

"The only way this fit work is through Aye transplant," the man said, his body seizing. "Find person wey deserve death so that you can deserve life."

Bode.

Bode's consciousness flitted in the old man's head, searching for the voice's origin. He looked back at the mirror to see the reflection, still like a mask. The old man's lips moved without Bode's control.

Rufus Adeyinka is my name. I be farmer inside Ogun state. I dey Lagos because of my sickness.

Bode's consciousness screamed, but there was no sound; the body did not move according to his will any longer.

No need shout, no one can hear you. Only me.

Who are you? Bode screamed, raw panic in his voice, unsure if he was paralyzed by fear or something else.

Me and my wife dey ojuju cult. I've been don try to cure myself in hospital but no work. You people are wicked, anytime I come, I wait for hours before you see me, your drug is expensive and you no care.

Bode began to remember. Rufus and his wife had been to the hospital before. He had attended to him but he could not afford the dialysis. He and his wife had begged him to reconsider, but he could not take people's personal problems on himself. He was not a messiah. So, he told them to go to another hospital or come back when they could afford to pay. When Rufus held the foot of his trousers, he had kicked his hands away.

Thank God say you remember, Rufus continued. *Me and my wife go to our ojuju cult and they say we should find somebody wey we fit exchange my life with—they call am Aye transplant.*

Bode's thoughts were no longer his alone. He could feel Rufus's consciousness mixing with his, assaulting his mind.

So na you we pick, because you wicked pass all the rest and nothing wey you fit do fit stop am, Rufus said, bursting into a cackling wave of hideous laughter that echoed in Bode's consciousness as he watched Rufus's reflection grin at him. *Enjoy your feem.*

Bode snapped out of the vile trance when the old woman shook him. Opening his lips, he called a name that was too familiar.

"Atinuke."

Bode's consciousness, shocked at the words leaving his mouth, watched as Atinuke moved closer to him, pressing her lips to his ears as Bode held his breath.

"The Baba said this will work, so do not worry."

"Where is the doctor?" Rufus continued.

The young man came to his side. Bode knew his name: it was Gbenga, the old man's only son, whom he had late in life. Bode's consciousness screamed, but the scream remained in the old man's head; Rufus didn't even acknowledge his existence. Atinuke held his hands and squeezed as the old man went limp. Bode's consciousness could swear that he saw Atinuke smirk.

Bode's consciousness watched everything unfold like a bad dream. He watched as his body, Dr. Bode, strode towards Rufus; how Atinuke got into her mourning wife character. As Bode walked over to him with his pulse oximeter, Bode's consciousness screamed at him.

"Run!"

There was no sound.

Bode's consciousness watched as Dr. Bode wrote in his documentation paper. Bode's consciousness kept watching, helpless, as he handed the paper to Titi, as Dr. Bode and Gbenga almost got into a brawl, and, finally, as Atinuke cursed him with vitriol. There was nothing he could do.

Bode's consciousness began to feel an insidious pull.

He woke up on the hospital bed to see Esosa seated on a stool, her head resting on what he could make out to be his thigh. She looked like she had not slept much, still wearing her dinner dress—a pink dress that shimmered against the fluorescent light. He had never seen this dress before. He opened his mouth to speak, but shut it, afraid that he would sound unlike himself. Bode tried to turn his neck, but felt a collar fastened around it. His movements stirred Esosa, who awoke and screamed for a doctor.

Esosa adjusted his pillow and smiled at him. She wondered how she would break the news to him that the truck driver who had rescued him, although having good intentions, had dragged him by the neck and destabilized his spine, and that Bode may never walk again. After the truck driver had called her, she took him to his hospital where his colleagues came to his rescue.

They reclined him on a hospital bed, taking turns pounding away at his chest. Nurse Titi was the first person to start compressions, while others gathered a defibrillator and a bag and mask. Each breath given after each compression seemed to suck the air out of the room as colleagues surrounded Bode, waiting for when Nurse Titi would tire so they could continue. They resuscitated him for thirty minutes before getting a weak pulse, finally taking him to the intensive care unit where he could be monitored.

When the doctor on call, Dr. Frances, had checked his X-ray, she had said that he would need spinal surgery.

"The surgeon on call is willing to do it for him for free because he is a colleague," she had said. Esosa was relieved because everyone in Bode's hospital had taken his

case like it was theirs; at least he had a fighting chance.

As she caressed his forehead, Bode wanted to speak, but felt tongue-tied. He attempted to move his limbs, but could not feel them. Red, orange, and yellow lights flitted before his eyes, settling on the lilac scrubs of the doctor examining him.

"We need to resuscitate him. Nurse! Bring a bag and mask!" she said, as she drew a curtain to shield him. "Please ma, I need you to step away from the bed." Off Esosa's horrified look, she said, "We will do our best, but God will do the rest."

Esosa did not believe in a god. Bode had once told her that doctors said such things when they knew there was nothing that could be done. Her heart leaped into her throat.

Bode could feel his eyes closing. He could see the colors in the room change from green to blue and indigo as he felt the same pull from before.

"I want to sleep," he muttered. Tears mixed with blood spilled down his cheeks as everything turned violet.

Bode moved when his eyes fluttered open to see a white light. He reached for the light and followed it until it led him to teeth; they were Esosa's teeth, but she was not smiling. He saw his limp body surrounded by Dr. Frances and other nurses taking turns giving him chest compressions. Titi restrained Esosa, who wrestled against her. There were tears in Titi's eyes.

"No! Don't leave me!" Esosa screamed, clawing at Bode's body like a feral cat.

He was in a white open space surrounding a central dark zone that swirled in violet and black colors. He watched Esosa through a portal that swished like an interdimensional window.

"Everything is going to be okay," he said, but she could not hear.

"Time have reach."

Rufus's voice could not be mistaken. He looked more vibrant than Bode remembered. An ache welled in Bode's chest, and he looked back at Esosa's face one last time as Rufus pushed him into the dark swirling void of nothingness.

Rufus opened his eyes to see Nurse Titi using a bag and mask to resuscitate him. He sprang up from his supine position and she backed away as Atinuke glided to him, her hands trembling as she touched his face.

"Oko mi," she said.

Rufus looked at her and smiled, flexing his fingers, feeling the new vibrancy of youth flowing through his veins like an infusion. "It is me."

     A DOSE OF INSIGHT

X
WHEEL OF FORTUNE

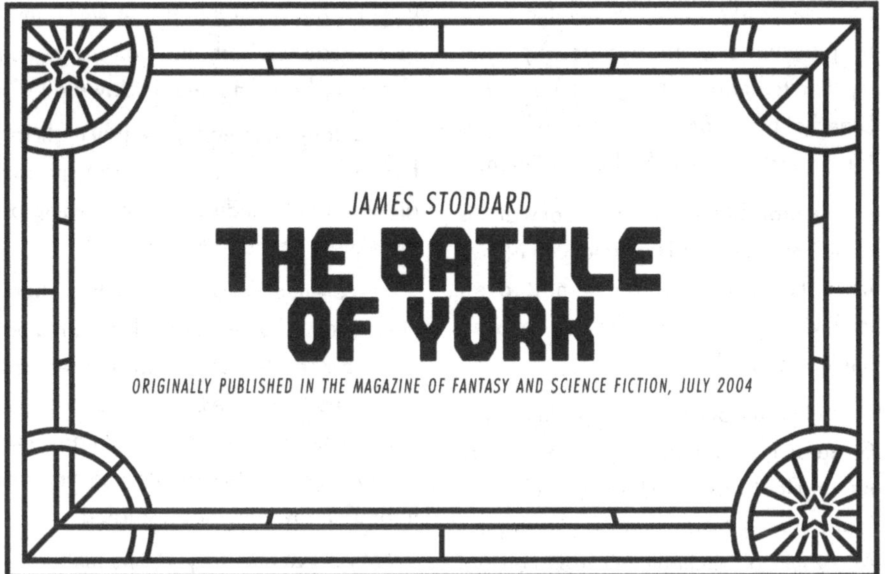

Three thousand years have elapsed since the passing of America.

Though scholars have uncovered multitudes of valuable archaeological evidence, little written literature exists from that era. It is indeed unfortunate that books made from paper were replaced by magneto-optical storage by the middle of the twenty-first century. The world-wide magnetic field disaster of the last decades of that century did more than herald a new Dark Age — it erased the literature and history of the world, even as the accompanying geological disruptions obliterated cities and landmarks.

Fortunately, near the end of the twenty-fourth century, an unknown scholar passed through the American regions, collecting the stories and legends that we now call "The Americana."

Though we can expect little accuracy from a people dependent on electronic data storage rather than oral tradition, we believe there is always a grain of truth concealed within the tales. But to quote one of the figures from the Americana itself: "When the Legend becomes fact, print the Legend."

☆ ☆ ☆

Young General Washington rode alone on his white stallion through the vast forest of Yoosemitee. His battle-axe, Valleyforge, hung glistening from the pommel of his saddle, the blood fresh-scrubbed from its edge. He had slain too many soldiers in the war against the Gauls and American Natives and was glad to be going home.

I will never fight again, he thought, *but will return to the Mount of Vernon to become a surveyor and farmer.* There was no pursuit more important to any country than to improve its agriculture and its breed of useful animals. How he longed for the simple cares of a husbandman.

He brooded on the horrors of war, his dead comrades, and the American Native maid, Pocahontas, whom he had loved. He loved her still, though she had betrayed him to the Gauls.

In his people's language, his name, General, meant pertaining in common to all, and that was what he had become, a leader to the American tribes in Virginia. As a youth, an enchantment had been laid on him by the Wise Woman, Betsee Ross, the Star Weaver, that he could never tell a lie. Because of this, some called him "Honest Gen."

As the last rays of twilight turned the ancient American forest golden with dust and sent the shadows streaming east, he heard the cry of the hawk and the distant howls of wolves. He shivered uneasily. The sequoias rose all around, hundreds of feet tall, the trees the American Natives called the Silent Giants.

His men had accompanied him through most of his journey, until he had chosen to shorten his trip by going through the woods. Even the bravest had refused to follow him then, for the forest was said to be haunted. At the time he had thought it just as well; he had wanted to be alone, to try to forget. He had intended to pass through the woods and into the safety of Virginia before nightfall, but weariness had overtaken both him and his mount, and in his brooding he had dawdled.

He dared ride no farther that night for fear of losing his way. Already shapes grew gray and indistinct. The howling of the wolves sounded nearer.

If I continue, I will lame Silver, he thought. He stroked the stallion's neck, then reined him to a stop. He dismounted, then led him forward a few paces, intending to make camp beneath one of the great trees. The shadows seemed to close around him. The hoot of an owl overhead startled him.

"My nerves are frayed," he muttered.

General removed Silver's bridle and saddle and let him go free. He was unconcerned about the stallion wandering off; the horse was as loyal as a hound. Silver nickered uneasily, as if he too distrusted the woods.

"Easy, boy," General murmured automatically. Though he preferred traveling unseen through Yoosemitee, he needed to start a fire to ward off the wolves. Picking up twigs and dead limbs, he soon had enough wood to last the night.

He knelt with flint and steel. Sparks flew and a tiny flame sprang up. Before he could fan it into a full fire, Silver nickered again.

General looked up, then stood, his hand to Valleyforge. A spectral green light haloed the enormous tree trunk. Washington crept around it and looked across the forest floor.

A man approached—a tall, inhumanly broad figure carrying a lantern that glowed with an unearthly luminance.

Washington felt his mouth go dry; his heart pounded against his chest, for he thought he recognized the intruder. He wanted to hide, but there was nowhere to go if the Pilgrim sought him. He drew Valleyforge and held it close. The figure paused a few feet from Washington. The lantern light spread at General's feet, turning the ground emerald and olive.

"General Washington," the figure said, his voice a deep drawl. "I am Waynejon. Some call me the Pilgrim."

"Have you come for me?" Despite General's best effort, his voice trembled.

The Pilgrim rumbled a laugh. "I'm not Death, if that's what you mean. I'm a man. I put my pants on one leg at a time."

Washington remained unconvinced. According to legend, the Pilgrim had died many times, but death could not keep him, for he was cursed to walk the earth until the end of the age because of an ancient wrong. He stood a head taller than Washington, who was a tall man himself, and wore a square, black hat with a buckle at its front, a black cloak, and ebony riding chaps. A black eye patch covered one eye and a rooster stood on his left shoulder. He carried an ancient blunderbuss.

"You look like you're getting ready to eat. If you'll share your fire, I have some salted beef in my pack."

General nodded, then finding his voice, tried to sound confident. "What brings you to the woods?"

"As a matter of fact, I've been looking for you."

☆ ☆ ☆

"And then," Waynejon concluded, "the boys got the cattle to the railhead."

Washington laughed and sighed. The fire crackled warmly before the pair. They sat across from one another, the flames between them. In the last hour, General had lost most of his fear. "An excellent tale. Whatever happened to the lads?"

"They turned out to be good men, most of 'em. But they're all long gone to their reward on Boot Hill by now."

In the subsequent silence Washington asked, "Why were you looking for me?"

"You get to the point. I like that."

The Pilgrim took a drink of coffee from a tin cup, then gestured with it toward the woods. "This country, this new land, it's wild, untamed. It could be a great nation, different from any other, a place where people could come from all over the world. A place of freedom."

"We all want that. It's why my forefathers came."

"Mine did the same. They fled the dark realm of the Old World to escape the tyrants. But it's not enough, General. The people aren't free."

"We've driven the Gauls back to France."

"But you didn't get Bone Apart, the Skeleton Man."

Washington shrugged. "He escaped to Mexico. No American can cross over the Rio Grande and live. An enchantment prevents it."

"He's done more than escape. He has made alliance with the Huns."

Washington drew a deep breath. This was bad news.

The Huns, led by their leader Hitler, the Wolf Prince, were a constant threat, raiding the coasts on their dragon-headed ships, striking and then fleeing. Was there never an end to peril?

"And it's not just Bone Apart and Hitler," Waynejon said. "There is a powerful wizard living in the dark regions of the Canadian north, whose heart is cold as the bitter winds that blow there. The Mounties can't stop him because he's conjured a giant from the Old World, tall as a mountain. They're climbing down the steep cliffs from the ice fields with their armies, preparing to march to York. The Huns, whose longships wait outside York Harbor, have promised the wizard great rewards if he helps them conquer America. The Gauls are reforming along the Rio Grande. We're in danger, General."

"What can we do?"

"Only the Words of Power in the iron box on Mount Rushmore can stop the giant. The titan has no strength against them."

"Mount Rushmore!" A chill ran along Washington's spine. "None have ever gone there and returned."

"It does not matter what others have done, General. I'm asking you."

"It was not my intention to seek further adventures."

"You gained a reputation in your battles against the Gauls."

"I heard bullets whistle, and believe me, there is something charming in the sound."

Waynejon laughed. "Sarcasm doesn't suit you."

"I meant none. By the miraculous care of Providence, I was protected beyond all human expectation, for I had four bullets through my coat and two horses shot under me, yet escaped unhurt. It was an exhilarating experience, but one I have little desire to repeat." He shook his head. "I fear you have chosen the wrong man."

"How do you figure?"

Washington hesitated, not wanting to say the words.

"My men love me, but though we seem to return from the war in triumph, it isn't true, at least not for me. I was the one who began the war against Gaul, when I urged the Virginian governor, Dimwiddie, to build Fort Necessity at the joining of the Ohio and Allegheny rivers. Had we not confronted the Gauls there, the colonies might have been spared much bloodshed. There should have been another way.

"Under my leadership, we struck out to attack Fort Duquesne. Though I knew better, out of my own vanity, we went like soldiers on parade, for I thought our movements were unknown. In my pride, I had told our plans to... someone... I cared for deeply, someone who betrayed us.

"We were unexpectedly attacked by three thousand Gauls and American Natives, and though our numbers were nearly thrice their own, my men were struck with such a deadly panic that nothing but confusion and disobedience of orders prevailed amongst them. We broke and ran as sheep before the hounds. If Braggart had not reinforced us at the end, the final battle would have been lost. Braggart himself, a mighty commander, was wounded behind the shoulder and into the breast. He died three days later. No, Pilgrim. I, a failure in all that I have undertaken, am not the man to perform this deed. You must place your trust elsewhere."

Waynejon took a long sip of coffee. "Seems to me that's the thing about this country, General. It's a land of second chances. Someone must go or America is lost."

Washington, who had ducked his head in shame, looked up into the Pilgrim's steady eyes and for a long moment, they held each other's gaze.

Finally, General murmured, "If I make the attempt, who will help me?"

"Near the slopes of Rushmore waits the Iron Hewer. Go to him. He will show you the way."

Washington stared into the fire and sighed. War had found him again and he could not refuse. Human happiness and moral duty were inseparably connected. "I suppose it is easier to prevent an evil than to rectify mistakes," he said. "I will set out tomorrow morning."

"That's good. That's mighty fine." Waynejon set his tin cup down. "I have to be on my way. Thanks for the grub."

Without another word, the Pilgrim rose and strode into the woods, his broad back disappearing into the shadows. Washington shivered, feeling very much alone.

☆ ☆ ☆

For seven days General rode through the forest of Yoosemitee, and on the eighth reached the wheat-covered plains of Kansas. The whole earth shook with the pounding hooves of herds of buffalo pursued by the valiant Comanches, who looked dreadful in their war paint. To escape their notice—for they had no love of the white man—Washington hid himself among the amber waves of grain.

At night, storm clouds built in the south and swept over the plains, the lightning tearing at the sky, the tumult of the thunder reminding Washington that should he survive Rushmore, he would have to face the wizard and his giant.

He crossed the country of Mount Ana, a stark land, all sky and earth, and came in the evening to the banks of the Little Bighorn, where sat a rider on a white horse caparisoned in midnight blue. The rider, too, who had a golden mustache and penetrating blue eyes, wore blue and gold, with a deep blue cape. His curling hair, falling down to the middle of his back, shone like ripe wheat in the sun. But Washington did not believe fine clothes necessarily made for fine men, any more than fine feathers made fine birds.

"Hurrah, good sir," the stranger called. "What brings you to the banks of the Bighorn?"

"I am Washington, who cannot tell a lie, a son of Virginia. I seek the Iron Hewer on the slopes of Rushmore."

"Then you seek death," the stranger replied. "I am Custard, named for the creamy white of my skin and my golden hair. I am called Arm Strong for my might, Lord of Horsemen, Captain of the Seventh Cavalry."

Washington perceived that this Custard had no lack of vanity, though he was indeed a mighty warrior. But General said, "I have never been to Rushmore before. Perhaps, if you know the way?"

"Why do you want to go there?"

"I seek the Words of Power to defeat the Wizard of Canada."

Custard gave Washington a long look before replying. "I will take you at least part of the journey, though I cannot tarry long. I have unfinished business here. The Sioux have risen against me."

Washington nodded. "I thank you for your kindness."

Together the two set off toward Rushmore. Along the way, Arm Strong told tales of his many deeds. Though he listened politely, Washington found such boasting distasteful, for it had always been his motto to show his intentions through his works rather than his speech.

"And someday," Custard said, "I will be the President of all this country, from east to west, and men everywhere will praise my name."

"I am unfamiliar with the word, president," Washington said.

"Like a king, but even greater, presiding as judge over the land."

"Perhaps, if the Huns and Gauls can be driven back," Washington said, thoughtfully, "but even a president should answer to the people."

"The people should answer to their liege lord, not the other way around."

"That is the old way, the manner of royalty," Washington said, as he stared out at the endless horizon. "Like all the dark necromancy of the Old World, it should best be forgotten. It will not be like that here. The purpose of all government, as best promoted by the practice of virtuous policies, ought to be the aggregate happiness of society. As the Pilgrim told me, America should be a place where everyone has a voice."

"You have seen the Pilgrim?" Custard asked.

"Yes. He was the one who sent me."

Arm Strong fell silent and dared brag no more of his own accomplishments.

After two days' travel, they reached the Black Hills of Dakota, where they rode through the gloom of perpetual twilight and eternal shadows, for the sun never shone in that dismal country. As they struggled through the gloaming, Washington spied a great eagle watching them from the back of the carcass of a bull buffalo, which the bird had apparently slain. As the travelers passed, General gave a respectful bow from his saddle and called out, "Greetings, Master of the Air. I see you will have a fine feast."

But the eagle only watched the men with unwinking eyes.

That evening, they came to a valley ringed in jutting peaks, and had traveled only a short distance when a cold voice called to them from the heights.

"Who dares trespass on the aeries of the eagles?"

High overhead, its talons clinging to the tallest peaks, stood an eagle twice the size of a stallion.

"I am Washington," General said, "with my companion Arm Strong, seeking passage to the Mount of Rushmore."

"This day, we will surely break your bones," the eagle screeched, "for I am E. Perilous Union, mother of the eagles who make their homes both in the Peaks of Usps and the Mountains of the Moon." Other, smaller eagles, lurking on the lesser crags encircling the travelers, raised their voices in agreement.

"Hear us, I beg you," General called, in as brave a tone as he could muster. "Spare us, not for ourselves, but for the sake of our mission, for we are on a journey for the freedom of our countrymen."

A ruffling of wings passed around the heights.

"Freedom!" E. Perilous cried. "Freedom! You speak the sacred word of the eagles. What is the meaning?"

"It is a word sacred to us as well," Washington replied.

"Mother," another eagle called across the heights. "Let us spare these men who speak of Freedom, for when I met them on the plains, the pale-faced one bowed and addressed me with respect."

"Is this so?" E. Perilous Union asked. "Tell us then, children of men, the purpose of your journey."

Washington did so, and when he was done, E. Perilous said, "We have heard of this evil wizard and despise his ways. Because my son, Apollo Leven, asks it, I will permit your passage. Moreover, in the sacred name of Freedom, I will send him as your guide."

Washington and Custard thanked the mother of the eagles, and Apollo Leven lifted himself above the crags to accompany them. As they continued through the Black Hills, wolves and evil spirits tried to destroy them, and more than once they battled for their lives, but Washington, his face grim and terrible to behold, fought with his great axe, Valleyforge, that shone silver in the darkness; and Arm Strong, wielding a golden blade, proved dreadful in combat. Apollo Leven strove beside them as well, and his terrible beak and talons slew many a foe.

The eagle led them true, and they finally saw Mount Rushmore looming in the distance, awful and majestic, a living monster shaped like a mountain with four heads. The heads were craggy and ill-formed, and shifted from side to side, guarding the treasure.

"The Iron Hewer lives at the base of Rushmore," Arm Strong said, "where the behemoth cannot reach him."

They came by twilight to a house made of iron. As they approached, a figure stepped out dressed in simple gray garments and bearing no arms. Around his bald head he wore a circlet with five silver stars that glistened in the dusk.

Washington expected to be challenged, but the man raised his hand in salute and gave a slow smile.

"Welcome, strangers, and be at ease. I am Eisenhower Iron Hewer, but my friends call me Ike."

Washington found he liked Ike immediately, and the two travelers dismounted and introduced themselves. When General told Eisenhower why he had come, the Old Commander shrugged.

"Though I have never liked war, I won't shirk from a fight, especially if Waynejon sent you."

From out of his larder, Eisenhower prepared a fine meal, though where he got his victuals Washington could not guess. Afterward, full and content, they sat before the hearth, drinking hot coffee and smoking tobacco from wooden pipes, listening to the wind whistling around the iron eaves, while Apollo Leven stood in a corner, his eyes reflecting golden in the flames.

"There is only one way to approach the creature," Ike said. "All its heads face south, except for the fourth one, which looks to the north. But that head is blind in one eye. If we're careful, we can creep up the northwestern slope. The box containing the Words of Power is hidden in a cave below the monster's chins. We'll know if it sees us, for its faces, which normally resemble rough stone, always take on the features of its victims."

"Can the monster be slain?" Custard asked.

"A single blow to the mountain's heart can kill the beast," Eisenhower replied, "if the warrior who delivers it is pure of soul."

"Who knows if such a man is among us?" Washington asked.

"I would like to try my hand at it," Custard said, "if the chance arises."

"Such a task is not for me," Eisenhower said. "I am unworthy. I've sent too many men to their deaths."

"Is that why you live here alone?" Custard asked. "A warrior such as yourself would be highly honored in York."

"I live here to serve and have had all the honors I need. I have led good men."

"You display great humility," Washington said. "Humility must always be the portion of any man who receives acclaim earned in the blood of his followers and the sacrifices of his friends."

"I have not fought for such, sir," Custard said, "but for the glory of combat. You give me much to consider. Still, I would like to set my good right arm against the monster."

"The Pilgrim sent me here many years ago, to act as a guide. There is a prophecy that one day a man will destroy the creature and use the Words of Power to preserve the land. I hope you are that one, but many have scaled those slopes. None have lived to tell of it."

"These are strange times," Washington said, "filled with magic."

"True," Ike replied, sagely, "but things are more like they are now than they have ever been before."

Washington nodded his head and stared into the fire. It was good to befriend a man of Ike's wisdom.

☆ ☆ ☆

The three companions rose with the morning light.

They left their horses in Eisenhower's stables and went on foot, angling toward the west, while Apollo Leven wheeled away to watch from a distance, lest his presence alert the four faces. If the monster saw them, it gave no sign. By midday they reached a region strewn with boulders, near enough that they could see the heads closely.

Washington gaped up at them. Three faced toward the men, one away. They were large as houses and all looked identical, with gray eyes, weather-beaten noses, and thin lines for mouths. Their guttural voices rose and fell, as they murmured among themselves in an ancient tongue.

The travelers headed north until they came to a point behind the mount, where only the easternmost face kept watch, its left eye staring vacantly down the slope.

"We begin the assault here, just before sundown," Eisenhower said.

"Shouldn't we wait until dark?" Arm Strong asked.

"No. They see as well at night as in the day, but at twilight the setting sun will be in their eyes."

For three restless hours, the companions waited for sunset, saying little, thinking of the coming encounter. Custard stared fixedly at the mount.

"Ike," Arm Strong finally said, "exactly where would the killing blow have to be struck? I cannot rightly determine the location of the beast's heart."

Eisenhower pointed. "There, just between the two central heads. Front or back makes no difference."

"And the Words of Power?" Washington asked.

"A few yards farther down in a narrow cave. It's hard to see from here."

"You have guided us well," Washington said. "You need not accompany us."

"I don't have to, but I will. I've always stood with anyone who made the attempt."

When the sun was still three finger-widths above the horizon, Eisenhower ordered the travelers to move out. They crept in between the boulders, keeping always to the blind side of the head, and were soon scrambling up the mountain slope. Pine trees provided concealment until they were two-thirds of the way up, but after that the mount lay barren.

Washington's heart pounded in his chest as he climbed. He tried not to look up at the terrible face above him. At first he could not see the cave, but then he spied it, a narrow opening half-covered by an overhanging shelf. If they could reach it, the head would be unable to see them.

Abruptly, the terrible visage turned with the sound of rock scraping on stone, and the three flattened themselves against the boulders, scarcely daring to breathe. For a moment the good eye swept along the slope, but the sunlight blinded it, making it squint and look away. The men kept climbing.

Custard was the first to reach the cave. He helped the others under the protection of the ledge. They clapped one another on the back and turned toward the opening.

It was little more than a niche in the rocks, and Washington searched only a short while before finding the iron box set in a recess. It proved to be neither long nor heavy, and he drew it out easily and opened the lid, which needed no lock with such a terrible monster guarding it. Within lay a brown parchment.

"The Words of Power," Washington whispered. He placed the scroll within his breast pocket and slipped the box back into its place.

"Have any ever come this far before?" Custard asked softly.

"Only two," Ike said. "Their bones are strewn across the slope."

Shuddering at Eisenhower's words, Washington told the Old Commander to lead them back down.

They were nearly to the tree line again before Washington realized that Custard was not behind him. He turned to discover Arm Strong ascending the mount. General clutched Eisenhower's shoulder and pointed to their comrade.

"That vain-glorious fool!" Eisenhower hissed.

Reaching the region above the monster's heart, Custard raised his sword high above his head, shouting, "Die, beast, in the name of Arm Strong, Captain of the Seventh Cavalry!" He looked magnificent at that moment, his cape billowing, his golden hair sweeping back behind his head, the last rays of the sun glinting on his blade.

With all his power, he thrust downward. The sword snapped beneath the weight of the blow, leaving Custard gaping at it in astonishment.

A scraping noise filled the heavens as all four of the monster's heads swiveled toward the captain. General gasped, for the faces had transformed into the features of Custard, Washington, and Eisenhower. Only the head with the blind eye remained unchanged.

The air filled with roaring as the heads screamed their rage. The whole mount trembled as vast arms rose from either side, reaching toward Custard.

"Let's go!" Eisenhower ordered. "He won't make it."

"No!" Washington cried, handing Ike the parchment. "Take it and flee!"

General did not hear Eisenhower's reply; he was already sprinting toward Custard, Valleyforge unsheathed. Though it had taken several minutes to creep down the mount, he ascended in seconds and was beside Arm Strong as the giant arms groped toward both of them. Washington saw his own face, filled with hatred, glowering down upon him.

Do I really look like that? he thought. *My nose seems so large.*

At that moment Apollo Leven streaked from the sky to harrow the faces with his talons. But the action bought the men only a moment before the rocks erupted around them, lifting them off the ground and sending them sprawling down the incline. Custard's expression was wild, but he held a knife in his hand as he rolled to his feet. Washington scrambled back toward the mountain's heart, axe upraised, staring straight into his own seething eyes.

The mount rippled beneath him, but as he fell he brought his axe down on his target with all his strength. He expected nothing but the destruction of his weapon, followed by his own death, but Valleyforge cut easily through the rock.

The whole mount screamed, a deafening blast. Blood rilled from the wound, covering General in ichor. He rolled on his back and saw the faces above him, including his own, writhing in their death struggles. He watched himself expire, the light leaving the eyes, the head lolling downward.

The mountain shuddered and sank. The four dead faces stared across the plain.

For a moment, Washington could hear nothing, but finally Custard's voice came to him, as the captain helped him up. "You have shamed me, sir, and saved my life. I am forever in your debt."

Eisenhower reached them a moment later and fell immediately to his knees before Washington.

"You are the one," Ike cried, taking the circlet of five stars from his forehead and casting it at Washington's feet. "The one who was to come. You have ended my vigil. Accept my service. Wherever you go, I will go also, and will serve you until my death."

"I too will follow you," Custard said, though he did not kneel. "Accept my service as well, General."

Scarcely understanding their words, Washington stared up at his defeated foe. "But how?" he exclaimed. "How could a failure such as I be worthy to destroy the beast when Arm Strong could not?"

Apollo Leven glided to a landing and placed his large head under General's hand. "Do not question the turn of events, Washington Paleface, but accept the fealty of these men, and mine as well, for I too would follow you."

Still overwhelmed, Washington laid his hands on the shoulders of the two men. "I do not understand, nor know where this will lead, but I cannot refuse the service of such brave warriors, nor of this great eagle. Now rise. We have a giant to kill."

"Another?" Ike asked.

They spent the night in Eisenhower's house, where Washington cleaned the blood from himself and his garments. In the morning they left Rushmore far behind, and the four dead heads gaped at them to the edge of the horizon.

☆ ☆ ☆

They rode once more across the darkness of the Black Hills, and as they went Eisenhower asked, "General, why did you go back for Custard? You had the scroll. If you and I had died, there would have been no one to stop the wizard."

"I could not leave him behind."

"If a commander thinks expending ten thousand lives will save twenty thousand later, it is up to him to do it."

"Custard was not ten thousand, but one," Washington said. "And though you have a point, I labor to keep alive in my breast that little spark of celestial fire called Conscience. I could not desert him and live with myself."

They passed back through Mount Ana, where Custard seemed to grow increasingly nervous. At last, they came once more to the banks of the Bighorn River, where they topped a hill and found a giant American Native standing before them. Behind him sat a man with the head of a stallion and another with the head of a bull.

"I am Bitter Gall," the native said. "The appointed time is come." He raised his arms and hundreds of warriors suddenly appeared over the hills, dressed in feathers and skins, war-paint covering their fierce faces.

Sweat broke across Arm Strong's brow, but he said nothing.

"What do you want?" Washington asked.

"Your people have sinned and there must be death," the sitting bull said.

"I have done it!" Arm Strong burst forth. "I am not what you think me, General. I admit it, now. I have shed the blood of children. I spoke before of unfinished business. Long ago, it was prophesied that I would meet my death by the banks of the Little Bighorn. I hoped to redeem myself in the slaying of Rushmore, but I failed there, too."

"Only one life is required," the stallion said. "One of you three. But none shall pass until the deed is done."

"I have accepted the fealty of this man," Washington said, "and I cannot tell a lie. I am responsible for him. I will accept the punishment in his stead."

For a moment, Arm Strong's eyes became crafty. But he looked at Washington and shook his head.

"No, General. I have been a villain, but you returned for me on Mount Rushmore when I would not have done the same for you. You must live to fight the wizard. My fate is sealed. You have shown me the way to restore my honor, and I will go with the sun shining on my face."

Custard bowed low to Washington, then strode down the hill toward Bitter Gall, passing out of the story and into history. But Washington wondered if someday he, too, would have to pay for the deaths of so many of his men in the battle of Fort Duquesne.

✩ ✩ ✩

Washington and Eisenhower, grieving at Custard's loss, made their way through the forest of Yoosemitee, where they had many adventures. At last, they came to York, a city of magnificent spires.

Others heard of Washington's heroism on Mount Rushmore, and warriors came to him offering him their service, so that he gathered a group of America's finest around him. Of these, Lafayette DeGaul was one of the greatest. Though a Gaul, he had vowed to follow Washington when General had saved his life many years before, and had been with him through the Gaul and American Native War.

"Mon General," Lafayette said, "it is good to see your face. The wizard, accompanied by his giant, approaches the city and is encamped beyond the banks of the Mighty Delaware. Those sent to stop it have been smashed to bits. I was just preparing to go myself, to die for the cause of freedom."

DeGaul was a wild-eyed man, with a mustache and plumed hat. Until he met Washington, he had been a member of the famous Musketeers, who had fought against the powers of darkness and evil in the Old World.

Washington assembled his company, which had grown to over five hundred men, just inside the gates of York. As he looked upon them, despair ran through him, for they were poorly armored and had little supplies, the Hun's blockade of the harbor preventing needed goods from entering the city. Despite his reservations, he drew a deep breath and addressed them briefly, explaining the situation.

He ended with: "The time is now near at hand which must determine whether Americans are to be Freemen or Slaves. The fate of untold millions will now depend, under God, on the courage and conduct of this army. Our cruel and unrelenting enemy leaves us no choice but a brave resistance or the most abject submission; this is all we can expect. We have, therefore, to resolve to conquer or die."

The men gave a ragged cheer while Apollo Leven wheeled and cried overhead.

Knowing how few warriors he had, Washington ordered a special surprise in the form of large, mysterious crates loaded onto the supply wagons.

As they rode out through the gates of York toward the Canadian Ice Fields, a crowd assembled to watch them go, young women pinning flowers and kisses on the warriors. Washington was approached by one of the most beautiful ladies he had ever seen, with pouting lips and eyes that flashed like fireworks. Her dark hair flared long and wild over a necklace hung with wooden teeth, suspended over a dress of forest green. She handed him a red, white, and blue standard covered with thirteen stars and stripes.

"Take this, General," she said, "and fight for York. The Star Weaver herself has enchanted it, washing it in the tears she sheds for those who die beneath the titan's heels. Tie it to your axe-handle in your moment of need, and its magic will give your blade power."

He reached down from the heights of Silver's back to take the cloth, and for a moment their hands and eyes met.

"What is your name?" he asked.

"Martha Custis."

"I thank you for this," Washington said.

She smiled and watched him ride away.

"She is a beauty, that one," Lafayette said.

"There is no time for such things," Washington replied, but his hand felt warm where she had touched it, and he raised the standard high.

✩ ✩ ✩

For three days the company traveled north and by the second afternoon, icy winds began to blow. Snow flurried at the evening and the warriors soon rode through banks of white. It was bitterly cold, and Washington's men lacked sufficient clothing.

By midafternoon, the company reached the edge of a valley, where ran the Mighty Delaware River. In the vale's center stood the giant, Britannia the Great, hundreds of feet tall, an enormous creature with the face of a woman, wearing a crown and carrying a heavy mace that it used to pound the earth. Wherever it walked or struck, it flattened houses, fields, and living things, a brutality that came to be known as the Stamp Act. The wizard stood upon the titan's shoulders and an army of ten thousand red-clad warriors followed behind.

THE BATTLE OF YORK

"How can we face them?" Lafayette asked.

"I have a plan," General said. "But the Words of Power will not work unless the monster hears them, so I must be very close. We will wait until nightfall."

The snow fell harder as evening progressed. The men carried half-shrouded lanterns, but it was still difficult to see through the storm. Everyone shivered with the cold, but Washington led them to the banks of the Delaware, accompanied by the wagon filled with the mysterious crates. They found boats upon the shore, left there at Washington's request by his American Native friend, Massasoit. In the dead of night, scarcely able to find their way, the company crossed the torrent of the Mighty Delaware, Washington standing upright, holding the red, white, and blue banner before him. He shivered from more than the cold, knowing that if the wizard or Britannia discovered them upon the waters, they would be doomed.

After a long hour, they reached the farther shore. Washington divided the men into three sections under the command of Eisenhower Iron Hewer, Ulysses Grant, and Benedict Arnold, three of his greatest warriors. Giving them their orders, General turned to Lafayette. "The rest is up to us, I fear. Come with me." Washington took the banner Martha Custis had given him and tucked it beneath his cloak.

Together, the two comrades crept toward the titan, whose gigantic form blocked the stars. They slipped through the sentries, then waited until moonrise.

As the first rays lit the land, Lafayette called in a loud voice, just outside the tent of the Wizard Cornwallis. "Come out, great magician, for we have seen your might and know we have no chance against you. Come and accept our surrender."

The sentries around Cornwallis's camp leapt to their feet, but Lafayette drew his bow and covered them.

"Stand back, my friends. We surrender to Cornwallis alone."

As the guards hesitated, the wizard appeared at the tent door, a dazzling lantern in his hand. Lafayette lowered his weapon. The wizard wore a bulky red robe and a white, pointed hood, which allowed only his dark eyes to show. His voice was grating as he spoke.

"Who dares interrupt the slumber of Cornwallis, Grand Wizard of the Empire?"

"It is I, Lafayette DeGaul, with the great General Washington, who asks you to accept his surrender."

The giant, Britannia, gave a low rumble and raised its mace, but Cornwallis bid it stay its hand.

"Why do you come slinking to me in darkness?" Cornwallis demanded.

"We came as quickly as we could, to end the bloodshed, for who knows what this behemoth of yours will do?" Lafayette replied.

Cornwallis laughed.

"I almost believe it. How like your people, the wretched refuse of the Old World, vermin sent to pollute these fair shores, fit to be nothing but slaves. When York is overthrown, I will show you how such should be treated."

"We are willing to do as you say," Lafayette said through gritted teeth. "Only accept our surrender."

"I have heard of you, Washington. It is said you cannot tell a lie. Answer me then, Commander, is that truly why you have come? I will believe it from your lips."

Washington dared not answer, knowing the truth would spring unbidden from his mouth.

"I thought so," Cornwallis said, signaling to the giant.

"Scatter!" Washington ordered. The Americans moved just in time to avoid a shattering blow, as Britannia brought its mace down with all its force. The impact tossed Washington off his feet, but even before he hit the ground he was unrolling the scroll containing the Words of Power, for this had all been part of his plan, to bring the giant close to the earth in striking. On landing, Washington instantly sprang up and began reading in a mighty voice.

At the first word, everything seemed to freeze in place, as if time had stopped. Britannia remained immobile as Washington spoke:

We hold these truths to be self-evident, that all men are created equal, that they are endowed by their

Creator with certain unalienable rights, that among these are Life, Liberty, and the Pursuit of Happiness. That to secure these rights . . .

On and on Washington read, his voice growing stronger with the reading, his delight rising as he saw the wizard and the giant both helpless against the words. He raised his arms as he ended:

And for the support of this Declaration, with a firm reliance on the Protection of Divine Providence, we mutually pledge to each other

our Lives,

our Fortunes,

and our sacred Honor.

The moment General finished, Cornwallis fell to his knees. When he tried to rise, Lafayette, with the speed of thought, raised his bow and placed an arrow through the wizard's evil heart.

"Liberty, Equality, Fraternity!" Lafayette cried.

Britannia gave a terrible scream, for the Words of Power began to turn its feet to stone. With a snarl, it fled toward the south, stomping away on increasingly clumsy members.

A roar rose from the valley's edge as hundreds of fireworks, the contents of the mysterious crates, were released at once. The sky erupted in red, white, and blue flares as Eisenhower, Arnold, and Grant led the Americans into the valley toward the Red Army, which was milling in confusion, stunned at being attacked from a direction they thought safe.

"The giant!" Washington cried. "It heads toward York."

Washington and Lafayette captured two of their enemies' horses and sped after the titan, but the mounts could not keep up. As soon as they reached their camp, Washington leapt off his steed and onto Silver, who stood waiting for his master, impatiently pawing the earth.

"Go on!" Lafayette shouted to Washington. "Go on, Mon General! I will catch up."

Faster than the wind, Silver ran, while Washington kept his eyes upon the giant. But when he reached the banks of the Mighty Delaware, General found the titan had already crossed. He nearly despaired at that moment, until Apollo Leven streaked out of the sky and landed before him.

"You must ride upon my back," the eagle screeched.

Still bearing the banner Martha Custis had given him, Washington climbed in front of Apollo Leven's wings. The eagle took a single bound and streaked over the great river.

Yet fast as they were, the monster strode far ahead. It steadily approached the gates of York, dwarfing the city's gleaming spires. Washington was still some distance behind it as it raised its mace, preparing to sweep the metropolis away.

In desperation, General lifted Valleyforge and tied the banner to its pommel.

As he let it fly, the weapon streaked toward the giant, the flag streaming behind, and as it flew it grew, powered by the flag's enchantment. It struck Britannia full in the back, and the monster writhed away, stumbling as it went, its massive feet missing the gates of York.

In its frenzy, it thrashed into the water. Most of its lower body was stone, and it moved with awkward, hesitant jerks. Crossing the bay, it pulled itself onto a massive rock rising out of the harbor. By the time it reached the top, its waist had turned to stone, leaving it unable to move its legs. Gradually the effect crept up its body. It raised its enormous mace in defiance and turned its face toward the sea, looking for its home across the waters.

Washington's axe, returned to its former size, fell from the giant's back and clattered down the rocks.

☆ ☆ ☆

With the giant and the wizard destroyed, the Red Army, thinking the fireworks the beginning of an enormous assault, fled in terror. Washington returned to his men and led them back into the city in triumph, the whole company singing *When General Comes Marching Home Again*.

Washington was declared a great hero and some wanted to make him king, but he refused, remembering Custard's words of a new office of president. He recalled what the Pilgrim said as well, and realized America was indeed a place of second chances.

The Gauls retreated from Mexico, and Hitler drew his boats back across the sea. Although Washington searched through all of York for many weeks, he found no sign of Martha Custis, nor anyone who knew her. However, he did find his axe with the flag still tied to its pommel, on the shores of the rock where the giant stood.

Afterward, a great Convention was held in honor of Washington's victory. A tremendous plan was conceived to build an enormous door, gilded with gold, across York harbor, to prevent the Huns from ever attacking again.

There was talk of tearing down the stone titan, but Lafayette had the last word. "Let it rather be a symbol, this vanquished foe. And we will call it Lady Liberty, for with its defeat we have won our freedom."

Being a poet as well as a warrior, in mockery of the words that the wizard had spoken, Lafayette etched the following lines upon the base of the rock where the giant stood:

☆ ☆ ☆

Give me your tired, your poor,

*Your huddled masses yearning
to breathe free,*

*The wretched refuse of your
teeming shore,*

*Send these, the homeless,
tempest-tossed to me.*

*I lift my lamp beside the
golden door!*

The Convention ordered a flame lit atop the statue's mace, that became a torch burning across the waters, so bright it could be seen from the shores of the Old World. And when the kings and emperors of that shadowy realm looked upon it, they trembled.

THE BATTLE OF YORK

VIII

OF PENTACLES

ORIGINAL HOME

Deep in the freshwater murk, there were once salamander-like creatures, six feet long and covered in clay. Vaguely human yet with tadpole tails. Like hellbenders, they found solace and sustenance in the mud. Their pale necks pulsed oxygen through slitted gills. Their eyes were triple-lidded. Their limbs were fleshy, water-wrinkled, and translucent.

There's a millennia-long metamorphosis happening; danger is the force that drives it on. From then to today, time carries the centuries like pocket change. Inside, the generations jingle-jangle. Entire communities live and thrive and die, an incessant chatter of forebears. All the while, our ancestors transform. Tadpoles to frogs. Our bodies transition from water to land.

Do we, deep down, still miss our original home?

The pregnant ones had anticipated this. And they worried for their children from the very start.

These rivers were no longer a good home for them. Something in the depths was stalking and stealing the young. Something in the mud was making them sick.

Refugees' homesickness is a special kind of grief.

Gathering up all the water they could, generations of pregnant mothers evolved wombs as watery as oceans. They swallowed up as much of home as they could. This kept the small ones safer, this kept them fed and protected. Then, when they were able, they fled forever from the dangers of the rivers. They held their breath as they plunged into the dangers of land.

God help me protect them.

Slithering onto the banks clutching their bellies, those first womb-wearers faced their first scorch beneath the sun. How strange it must've been, to see the sogginess disappear from their skin. How brave of them to make such a change. We've always been explorers. But, I'm not sure if the changes we've made since carry the same weight. I'm not sure if we still carry enough water with us.

We have since settled in many different places across the universe, on so many planets with a variety of ecosystems, each lifestyle impacted by varying atmospheres, threats, and levels of humidity. As we fled this way and that, our genes pooled and congregated and mixed. Here and there, potential opportunities for evolution's creativity opened and closed. Somehow, in all the chaos, my ancestors carried their inheritance, here, to one of the driest planets.

The view from my potting bench in the Botanical Dome is one marked only by ancient water. Where a thunderstorm's chisel would create negative space on Earth, here, the rocks stand erect and unmolded. There is no rain to erode rock into river-canyon. Here, there is only the primordial sculpture of planetary process.

Of upheaval from below, of a different kind of battering from the elements. The sandstorm wind flecks all the surfaces with tiny holes. There is no pottery-like smoothness in these landscapes. We have long left those fluvial curves behind. Things here are rough. And the air is too dry to breathe.

The Domes' humidifying system meets its requirements of keeping us alive, but I still find cracks in my skin. They said, with my appetite, I would be happier working in the Botanical Dome. I get to handle the hoses and spraying mechanisms. I keep the crops alive. I mist the seeds until their heads rise through the soil. I water them until they bear fruit. Then, I watch as the plants take to their rations as unkindly as I do. Their green is ghostly long before their spirits are ready to leave. They pallor and wilt.

It seems the plants know a similar suffering and have changed due to it, too. To alleviate their pain, I try to be consistent in my waterings. I don't take any for myself, though the temptation is strong. I down my day's water rations long before evening. I go to bed dry-mouthed and yearning. My dreams are full of water.

Submersions.

Those first womb-wearers would return often to bodies of water with their offspring. Lakes and oceans, rather than rivers. In those early days, you could find them submerged together, their lengthening hair splayed out like jellyfish whispers in the water. Generations away from shedding their extra eyelids, they'd dip in until they were eye-level with the water's surface, dividing their pupils into above and below. They'd stare, unblinking, through the film of their own skin. In that fashion, they'd soak and soak and soak.

I don't like the direction we're going in.

"You think about water more than most people," Irene told me after work one day, her eyes red-rimmed, her lips chapped.

It disturbed me, how her water ration thermos always felt full. How she didn't seem to notice the sandpapery texture of her tongue.

"Honestly, babe. Your behavior is starting to concern me," she was saying. As she squeezed my hand, her hand-skin crackled. "I've set up an appointment for you with Dr. Jimenez."

There had to be someone like me among the first of them. I must have retained one of their genes. While everyone in the Domes settles like stones in this drier world, I can't help but imagine swimming. As I savor my sips, feeling the liquid roll over my tongue and coat the roof of my mouth, I imagine the satisfaction of a bigger gulp. To feel a stream run down my throat. To open my mouth wide and feel no end of it. Endless water, to drink until I'm satisfied, my belly bursting and round enough to bear life.

We need to go back.

There is an unspoken rule around here: do not stare at the mirage.

The mirage is visible in all directions, along the horizon. It shimmers there, like the shine off a distant lake. It shimmers with the glimmer of a need fulfilled. It makes promises like a magician. There is the illusion of cool, hydrating depths in the distance. I try not to stare too long at it. But there are days, my thirstiest ones, where I find I've zoned off. My eyes have become enraptured.

In the waiting room outside Dr. Jimenez's office, I stare at the mural that memorializes those we've lost to the mirage. There are hundreds of names, painted by a steady hand. Most of the names are from many generations ago, long before most people changed.

Adaptation is a kind of change.

Dr. Jimenez reminds me of a succulent, simultaneously plump and resilient. I am jealous of the way she retains her water. Her skin is strong, not flaky. Her eyes gel-over in their sockets. Moisturized. A comforting glisten. Her cells are doing something right.

"Swish and spit," she tells me, handing me a plastic cup. I look at her, I look at the cup. My mouth parches at the thought.

"What if I don't want to?"

She smiles kindly at me and opens her ration bottle. She pours an ounce of water into it and offers me the cup once more. I take it. I swish, my tongue absorbing almost all of it immediately. I spit a fraction of what I was given and hand it back.

She takes the cup from me without comment. She pipettes my sample from the cup and dispenses it into a port at the base of her palm-sized device. She clicks and prods at the buttons, staring at the screen.

"Oh," she says, nodding. "Your obsession with water makes sense."

She turns the screen toward me, my genetic sequence highlighted in a couple of key regions.

"You are a descendant of the last of the Womb-Wearers."

God help me protect him.

I have a child growing, but not within me. I go to visit him as often as I can. He is arranged with the rest of them, in free-standing amniotic capsules. Within, he is suspended in a thick, nutrient-dense gel. I wonder how such an immobile, isolated beginning is affecting him. I wish I could keep him within me, as our ancestors did. But they say we simply couldn't spare all of that extra fluid. Once fluid is within a human body, it requires more maintenance. More bookkeeping, tallying, tracking. And some of it always vanishes. Our humidifying system can't seem to recapture all of what we sweat, the steam that rises from our throats with speech. Try to speak aloud less, they say. That is what our communication platforms are for.

Is there a gene for a tendency toward nostalgia? Too often, I imagine waves lapping at my feet, the sizzle *shhhhh* sound my skin would make as I am immersed. Finally. What a relief. I imagine holding a child's hand, guiding them through the turbulent waves, explaining the cycle of a tide.

There must've been one among the first of them, a hundred generations after the beginning of the land-living, to feel disturbed by all the changes. Perhaps the thing that disturbed them was how we could no longer breathe underwater. They would gasp in their grass-cushioned sleep, remembering the weightlessness of underwater existence.

Ancient movements would resurrect themselves within the throes of their slumber. Half-awake, they must've clawed at their throats, felt the stitched-up-gill-slits and felt a brief panic for breath, before remembering their lungs. When they comforted themselves with a visit to the cove the following day, they must've wondered what wonders they've lost with the shortening of their tails. As their digits became less webbed, as their extra eyelids were absorbed by their orbits, maybe they started to see the water as less and less friendly. Maybe the land became more and more of a comfort.

Who are we becoming?

The creation of milk was a form of blood-alchemy that strengthened the blood bond between children and their parents. But our blood is too viscous for such transformations, now. There is barely enough to keep us moving. So many of us stay still for much of the day. Most of us complete our duties by sending drones labor-codes. Intaking and releasing almost nothing is a good way to conserve resources. People are becoming more and more like succulents and stones.

I guess I'm anachronistic. I drink my rations hungrily and, though I'm not pregnant, I've retained a hope of breastfeeding. It's more of a fantasy, an unattainable wish. I've taken to swallowing my day's final sips before the bathroom mirror.

When all is through, I squeeze my nipples, hoping to see milk. There is still a part of me that yearns to bond with my boy in the old-fashioned way. They say we'll bond just fine without it, that breastfeeding is impossible by now. Something deep within me rebels, quakes. There is a deep sense of grief.

Evolution molds relationships as well as bodies.

In the Botanical Dome, the delicate stems of the saplings I care for need to be handled by a soft, knowing hand. Gently, they are laid down into burrows of compost. Transplanted into new soil, they can learn what it means to continue growing. I must help them. On this planet, they cannot do it on their own.

At the very end of my son's third trimester, he'll be transplanted into my arms. Together, we'll cry without tears, as is the modern fashion. We are an endangered breed, he and I. The thirsty ones. The ones who savor our water. The ones still connected, by a vital urge, to our ancient origins on Earth. Sure, maintaining this connection equates to a lifetime of suffering. But there is no life devoid of suffering. I'd rather he move, I'd rather he utter words. If he must thirst, I'll be there with him, to speak the unspoken:

Son, look away from the mirage, now. It's going to be alright.

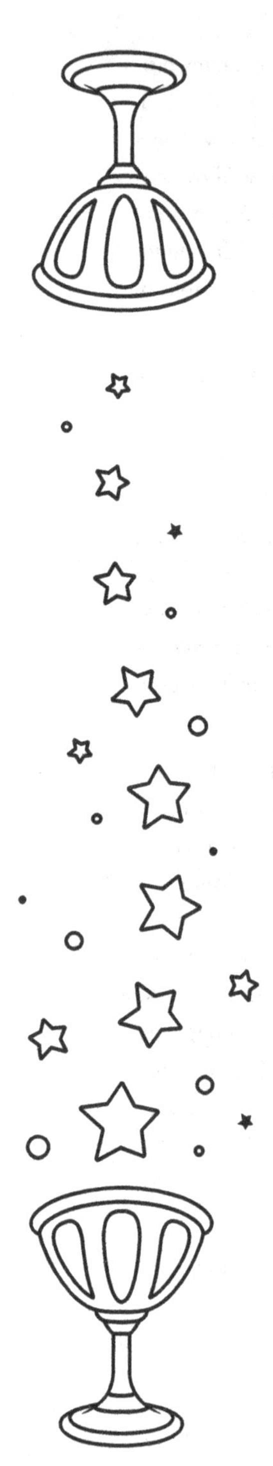

VI
OF SWORDS

You've been tailing a ghost since midnight, across a gray, rocky plain under a broken moon.

As the ghost walks, it sheds pieces of joy like scales from a serpent. The ghost is a woman, and she is kicking up dust and humming to herself.

As you follow her across the cold lava field, remnants of old memories come back to you: the neighbors who helped you hide when the whole world wanted to kill you. Strange music in the dusk filtering up through the houses like a floral fragrance you couldn't quite place. Food stuff, nearly inedible but still a salvation, left in boxes for you at the door. The texture of a soft curtain beneath your fingers as you peered out a window, willing yourself invisible, while the square filled with smoke from the burning of human things.

Your feet slip in the dust, and shards of basalt fill your socks and cut your toes. The woman stops in the trough of two hills where hot molten once flowed several hundred years ago. Her outline is bright with the setting moon. She searches for something with the toes of her boots. Then she kneels at the base of a small hillock and begins to dig.

You crouch and watch her and think about that bonfire in the square on that other planet where you were born, and a man, like you, whom they dragged out to it clutching a small blue ceramic bowl to his breast, as if it might keep him afloat in the sea rage. Who knows what the bowl meant to him?

Your heart beat like a trapped bird as you watched them disassemble him. The flames consume his pieces, and his flesh peels from his bones, and his clothes turn to char.

You could only hope that the people who were hiding you would not be inspired to turn you out. One of them was out there in the square, watching, their strange, carapace-covered face bent in an expression you knew to mean anger, and all you had then was that frayed strand of faith in the instinct of life to protect other life, same species or not. You heard the collective cry as a vibration in that pane of glass beneath your palm.

You were born human on a lush violet planet, child of a people brought in to mine the soft minerals out of narrow tunnels in the cave. At school, the other children liked to watch you manipulate clay into small flowers and insects. What they liked were your little, dexterous fingers and your double-knuckle opposable thumb. You were shorter than all of them. They had to bring in a separate set of furniture just for you and your crude, bipedal form. As a child, you were treated kindly. The people of the violet planet prized children above all, and that is what saved you later from the Extinction.

The ghost is digging frantically, now, in the loose dirt. The thing she wants is not there. She rises and crosses to the other side of the shallow dip in the field and begins to dig again.

You can hear her voice saying, "No, no, no," and your heart squeezes with synchronous anxiety out of habit.

There was a vote by the High Council that year, that humans were no longer desired for mining. Mining, in fact, was evil. It defiled the ground and clogged the air. And the humans who did it were dirty and sly and destructive. The humans must be expelled.

For weeks, traffic to the shuttleport clogged the sky. All humans with means were trying to leave. Your family had no money, and so you were still there when the new law came the following year that, as humans were no longer productive members of society, it would be best to eliminate those that remained.

You remember sitting between your parents on the mattress and hearing this over the public link, and the tears that ran down your parents' faces as they pressed you close and kissed your head. That night, they bundled you into a large pot with a heavy lid, and they delivered you to your neighbors' house—the one with a human-style garden in the back with flowers and tomatoes that would soon be torn up to diffuse any suspicion. That was the last time you saw your parents.

The ghost sits panting in the dust. At last, she sees you.

"Who are you?" she asks, her skin a shadow in the cool starlight.

"No one important," you say. "I live in town just back there. I saw you out my window as I was going to bed."

"I've never seen you before," she says, eyes narrowing.

     GHOSTS IN THE ASH

She comes closer, closer to you, reaches out and touches your face with her skin-covered fingers and at the same moment, you both realize the other is alive and real. You so rarely see other humans these days, even though it is not a crime. She smiles in wonder, and you feel your face respond with unfamiliar muscles. You feel suddenly buoyant. You are glad you came.

There was one close call, when police came and searched the house, so soon after a previous inspection that you were not hidden in the eaves. The child of the family hiding you came running in and pushed you roughly down and rolled you up in a piece of cloth like the cigarettes your parents used to smoke. You heard the heavy clacking on the stairs. The child kicked you, so you rolled back against the wall and had to bite your lip against the pain of it. You did not know whether their child understood how soft and breakable you were, or if the injuries were punishment for the ever-present fear that hung over their home. The child never played with you, or even seemed to like you much.

The police came into the room and began to question the child. They began breaking things loudly, and you were amazed the child did not make that high-pitched hum that meant sorrow and regret.

All the while you lay there, practically in plain view, glad that their hearing was not as good as yours, because your breathing was louder than an orchestra in your ears. At last, the police left, and the child unrolled you.

"We are safe," they said.

And you thought, was that a mistake? We? Because you had never been referred to as one of them, and it filled some hole in your chest you did not know was there but also somehow made you more afraid. You wanted to hug them then, but you knew better than to impose such a human gesture on a person all bent limbs and shell and sharp edges. All you could do was hug yourself.

You do not know this woman, but you help her anyway, dig in the dust for hours. She is looking for a box of contraband seeds that her parents hid out here. They need not have. On this planet, homes are not searched regularly by the police. And now she has lost her heirloom: the hope of curling vines of squash, fragrant lemon trees, and blueberries on the bush. You would like her to find these things, but there is nothing in the great field of ash that gives away its secrets.

The box could be anywhere, and the sun will be rising soon.

"It's all right," she says. "I found you at least." She smiles again.

It took five years for the Extinction to end. Two years before that, you managed to leave the planet and come to another one that still hated you, but hated you less. You learned how to sew their clothes with a machine, and the way the scissors sounded as you snipped cheap fabric into pieces made you feel whole. You thought of those people who did, in the end, love you, not *you*, but the sacred possibility of you and who you could be in another place.

When the sun rises, you and the woman agree to give up. You clasp hands for a moment, and then walk back across the powder fields as the heat of the day begins to rise. You return to the small apartment you rent near the main street. You can hear the soft rumble of shopkeepers greeting each other as they set up their displays.

You set a pot of water on the stove and sprinkle it with dried herbs for a tea. You shut your eyes and feel the light through the open window begin to fill you up. The pot begins to bubble, and the smell of it fills your nose, bitter and deep. That is how you know you are you, and here, still here.

II
OF WANDS

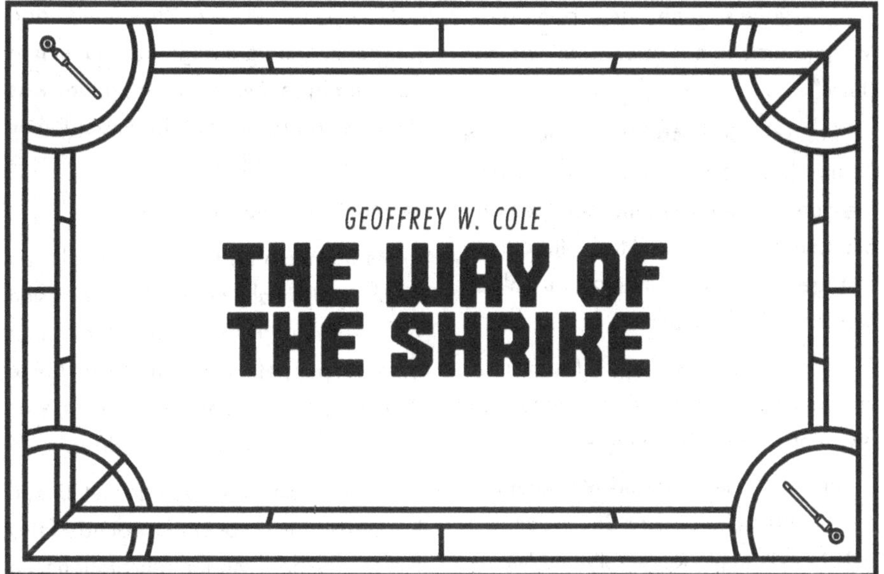

Every time their potbellied house demon admitted another guest to her birthday party, Marjormam hoped that it would be Pranny. Every time it wasn't, Marjormam fed her disappointment another hors d'oeuvre.

The house filled with friends from school, teachers, aunties and uncles whose names Marjormam couldn't remember, all of them telling her how proud they were that she would be joining her father on the spike. *I'll never go on the spike*, she wanted to tell them, but their plan was a secret, so Marjormam kept her mouth filled with pigeon-meat pastries.

Soon it was time to put on their show, and Pranny still hadn't arrived.

"Can you do the show on your own?" her father asked from outside the washroom in which Marjormam had locked herself.

"It's a two-person musical, Dada."

Out in the entryway, the house demon growled in welcome.

"Relis, Franco, Pranny," her father said, loud enough that Marjormam could hear. "So glad you could make it!"

Marjormam dabbed at her eyes with her lace sleeve and slid out of the washroom as if she'd never heard of the place.

"Sorry we're late," Pranny's father Relis said. "Pran couldn't decide what to wear."

All the careful nonchalance Marjormam had composed fled when she got her first look at Pranny. The dark black dress she wore was so tight it might have been painted on.

"Hey kiddo," Pranny said, wrapping up Marjormam in a chaste embrace. "Happy Childhood's End."

Perfume drenched Pranny's bare neck, hiding something sour beneath the musk.

"Everyone's in the living room, girls," Marjormam's father said. "Think we can start?"

That snapped Marjormam out of her Pranny-haze. She dragged Pranny past the guests crammed onto couches and dining room chairs, and they slid behind a stage the house demon had unfolded in front of the fireplace.

"What took you so long?" Marjormam whispered behind the stage. "There are a few scenes I wanted to talk—"

Pranny kissed her and Marjormam's complaints melted away. She moaned in delight as Pranny's tongue slipped into her mouth, but as she ran her fingers along the hem of Pranny's dress, Pranny released her and launched into vocal warm-ups. The taste of hot wine lingered on Marjormam's lips.

Pranny passed her the Dread Baroness puppet and whispered, "Our audience awaits."

"Pran," Marjormam said. When she slid the puppet onto her hand, the panicked thrill of the impending performance set her heart racing. "It's really happening. By this time tomorrow we'll be on the road."

Pranny tucked a piece of paper into Marjormam's sleeve. "A few more things to pack before we go. If you can't get them all by the end of my shift, that's okay, we can wait another day or two."

No, Marjormam wanted to say. She couldn't wait another day or two—tomorrow night would be her first on the spike—

but Pranny raised the Brother Daedledoo puppet into the ghostlight and launched into an old revolutionary song that was the opening number of the musical they had written together.

Well, not entirely together.

Marjormam had wanted to write an autobiographical show, but Pranny insisted on performing history, like all the other amateur puppeteers around town. Once they were on the road, Marjormam was sure Pran would listen to her ideas.

Forty-five minutes later, the felt Dread Baroness loomed over the wounded Brother Daedledoo. Marjormam pronounced the verdict: "For trying to steal the land of my ancestors out from beneath my feet, yours shall never touch it again. I condemn thee to eternal torment on the Spike."

The living room erupted in applause. Marjormam hated performing for relations: you never knew if the adulation was sincere or simple flattery. The road would be the true test.

After the last of the guests filed out, Marjormam's parents insisted she go to bed.

Marjormam handed Olbert the house demon a pair of sticky ice wine glasses. "I'll help Olbert. I don't think I can sleep yet."

Before Mama could protest, Dada put a hand on his wife's shoulder. "They call it Childhood's End for a reason, dear. She gets to make her own decisions now." He patted Marjormam's cheek the way he'd done since she was a little girl. "You're on spike 12492 at seven p.m. It's far, but you'll be promoted closer in no time with your acting skills." He gave her a warm embrace. "You're going to do so well."

Only after the sounds of her parents' bedtime routine quieted did Marjormam open the note Pranny had given her. The list was extensive. More food, more wine than Marjormam imagined they could carry, and there, at the bottom of the list, a pair of matching corsets. Corsets. Even the finest corseterie in the City required a couple days to complete their craft after taking measurements.

Marjormam crushed the list in a sudden fury. After "Take Your Kid to Work Day," almost four years ago now, she'd sworn she would never mount the spike. Even then, she'd known she wanted to be a puppeteer. Pranny knew that better than anyone. Pranny had her first shift two months ago when she turned seventeen, and every time they got together, Pranny told her how awful it was. How much she wanted to get away. Yet Pranny's list practically guaranteed Marjormam would be on the spike tomorrow.

Olbert handed Marjormam a handkerchief. She thanked the twisted creature and enlisted his help in folding up the stage and loading it with supplies. Once loaded, she hefted the stage onto her back. The straps dug into her shoulders, but it wasn't that bad, and there was room for more.

Find matching corsets, she thought, lying in her childhood bed for what she told herself was the last time. *Find corsets, and then we're free.*

The City's ten thousand vultures circled down through the fading daylight to roost. As the clock ghosts moaned six o'clock, Marjormam staggered under the weight of the stage onto the Way of the Shrike. She didn't have long: Pranny's shift ended at seven, and they planned to hit the road from there.

On either side of the Way, men and women writhed on their spikes. As a new spikeperson, union rules dictated Pranny was impaled far outside the city, almost four kilometers from the gates. Omnibuses took spikepeople out to those distant sites of perpetual torture, but Marjormam had spent the last of her coin on the matching corsets carefully strapped to the outside of the folded stage, so she had to walk.

Marjormam pulled her cloak over her head as she approached her father's spike. She would have said goodbye to her parents if she thought they'd let her leave. Instead, she'd left a note with Olbert, and strict instructions to deliver it tomorrow when she failed to return from her shift.

It seemed much longer than an hour later when the clock ghosts moaned seven. Pranny's shift was done. Marjormam swore, and started to run as best she could under the weight of the folded-up stage. She crested a hill and spotted Pranny, still impaled on spike 10957 on the roadside ahead.

The spike had erupted through the soft flesh above Pranny's right breast, tearing the skin that Marjormam so adored. She hung pale and trembling beneath the gore-covered shaft, her legs kicking in the air a hand-width above the gravel. Marjormam was about to run the last few paces when she noticed the girl standing at the base of Pranny's spike. A few years older than either of them, the girl wore fishnet stockings, cap, and corset, her entire outfit stained and torn from a shift on the spike, though her flesh was whole.

"It's okay, Pran," the girl said. Pran? Only Marjormam called her Pran. "The barbers will be here soon. You're almost done."

Jealousy burned hot down Marjormam's veins. She slid the stage off her shoulders and ran to Pranny's side. As she was reaching out to touch Pranny's twitching legs, the older girl said, "Don't touch her."

Marjormam pressed her hands to the cold, tacky skin of Pranny's thigh. "It's going to be—"

Pranny's eyes widened in alarm.

"Don't touch me!" she screamed.

Marjormam reeled away as if struck. She pressed her hand to her mouth, tasted Pranny's semi-congealed blood, and she almost vomited. Everything happened so fast after that. A young man in a red-and-white striped shirt arrived at the base of Pranny's spike, and when he squeezed a few drops of clear fluid onto her tongue, she went slack.

Now the older girl touched Pranny's face, brushed the sweat-damp hair out of her eyes, and whispered things Marjormam couldn't hear. A twisted little demon that looked like a hairless goat who'd had its forelimbs swapped with a monkey's cranked a mechanism at the base of the spike. Over half a minute, Pranny rose up the length of wood that she had spent a cruel thirteen hours descending.

When she neared the top, the older girl and the barber leaned a ladder against the spike and, working together, carried Pranny down to a waiting leather bedroll. The barber poured an aubergine-colored liquid between her lips. Seconds later, the wounds marring Pranny's shoulder and fundament closed up, color seeped back into her flesh, and her breathing came easy. She sat up.

The older girl produced a wineskin that Pranny pulled on for a long moment. The older girl offered it to Marjormam, but she refused.

"Sorry," Pranny said. "It's very hard at the end."

"It doesn't matter," Marjormam said. "You won't ever have to mount the spike again. I've got everything ready. Even the corsets. They're off the shelf, but we're about the same size, and they fit me well. We can put them on when we get to the campground at Flayton."

     THE WAY OF THE SHRIKE

Pranny exchanged a glance with the older girl. Marjormam felt her chest tighten. Pranny seemed about to say something, then stood and brushed flecks of gravel off her gore-stained clothes.

"We can't go yet," Pranny said, speaking more to the older girl than to Marjormam. "I have to get changed before we hit the road."

Marjormam patted the side of the stage. "Our clothes are packed. We'll stop at the first waystation and you can wash up there."

Again, that considering look with the other girl. "And I have to collect my pay." Pranny took the stage and swung it onto her shoulders. She made the whole operation look so easy. "We're going to need all the money we can get. Come on, Marjie, we can take the omnibus back into the City."

Pranny offered Marjormam a blood-flecked hand. Marjormam looked back down the Way of the Shrike with its forest of impalees toward the City Infernal. This was the furthest she had ever traveled without her parents. A part of her whispered that if she turned back now, she would never leave again.

"We can try on the corsets once I'm cleaned up," Pranny said.

But that was a silly thought. She had walked this far, surely she could do so again. Marjormam took Pranny's hand.

A serving demon tottered down the aisle of the omnibus carrying a multi-layered tray of confectionery and beverages. The older girl, who'd introduced herself as Seferia, bought bladders of wine for her and Pranny, bubble tea for Marjormam, and a sack full of pastries they all shared. Covered in icing sugar, full of caffeine and alcohol, Marjormam and Pranny sang bits of songs from their show for Seferia, who clapped after each snippet. The dread that had taken root in Marjormam's belly as the omnibus rolled back into the City was easy to ignore when she was in the company of these two beautiful women, the weight of the folded-up stage no longer digging into her shoulders. They would still leave, she kept telling herself, in the quiet moments between bursts of song and laughter.

"Why don't you get off at Chiropractor Square," Pranny said. "The paymaster's is another few stops further on. I'll come back and meet you there."

"Like the old song," Marjormam said.

"'Met my love 'neath the Gallows Tree,'" Seferia sang.

"'I was swinging,'" Pranny and Marjormam sang in harmony, "'and she was free.'"

All three of them exploded into laughter.

Seferia put a hand on Pranny's forearm, the touch so intimate that Marjormam barely registered what the older girl said: "I think you need to tell her, Pran."

The bubble tea seemed to go sour in her gut. "Tell me what?"

The bell rang and the conductor demon called out, "Chiropractor Square! All connections."

"That this is your stop," Pranny said. "Hurry, Marjie, or you'll miss it."

Marjormam ran to the door and had stepped down the stairs when she realized she'd left the folded stage on the bench. "The stage!" she shouted at Pranny and Seferia. "I forgot the stage!"

She argued with the conductor to get back onto the omnibus, but the driver was already whipping the dromedaries into action. As the great vehicle pulled away from the curb, Pranny appeared in the doorway, stage held awkwardly in front of her. Marjormam took it, staggered under the weight, and fell away from the omnibus to land with a thud on the hard cobbles. Wood cracked. A peal of laughter echoed from behind her, as if everyone in the Square found her misfortune hilarious, and embarrassment ignited the jealousy coursing through her veins as she rolled out from beneath the stage.

But the laughter wasn't for her.

A crowd was watching a puppet show on the far side of Chiropractor Square and they now booed as a puppet, who had to be the Wild King Daedledoo, pranced about the stage. The omnibus disappeared down one of the City's cavern-like streets. Marjormam hoisted the stage up, and swore as bundles of smoked pigeons tumbled out of a crack in the frame.

She dragged the stage over to a bench beneath the soaring limbs of the Gallows Tree and tied a strip of ribbon around the cracked frame. Dead criminals hung from the branches of the old tree, and the carrion monkeys who called the tree home feasted on the thieves and back-alley circumcisers and false prophets who had met with the Dread Baroness' justice.

Marjormam ate one of the smoked pigeons, hoping the food would calm her, but with every bite, she imagined the declaration Pranny had left unspoken. Was Pranny planning on leaving with the older girl instead? Or perhaps she wanted to propose? Maybe she wanted to perform as the Dread Baroness and relegate Marjormam to the First Spikeman role. Yes, that had to be it.

Marjormam watched the puppet show from the bench. She squirmed at the similarities between the play and the one Pranny had written. Pranny's show treated the history of Daedledoo's Revolution as the most serious drama, whereas the performers across the square turned the whole thing into a farce. Despite herself, Marjormam laughed at a few of the jokes. Thousands had died during the revolution and in the centuries of impalements that were its legacy, it shouldn't be funny, but the crowd lapped it up too. They should try to make their show funnier, Marjormam decided.

She rested her head against the bench as she watched, and she didn't even notice when exhaustion dragged her down into sleep.

THE WAY OF THE SHRIKE

A woman's voice woke Marjormam. "Shoo! Get away, filthy things!"

Marjormam blinked as she sat upright. "Pranny?"

"Oh, thank the countless stars," said the woman in a Wildlander accent. "We thought you was dead." The woman standing above her was older even than Seferia, and had sad green eyes that shone in the ghostlight. "It's late, child. You ought to be getting home."

"I am not a child," Marjormam said. "And I'm not going home. I'm leaving the city tonight."

"The monkeys may have ruined those plans."

The stage lay on its side, its contents spilled across the dirty cobbles. In the dark branches of the Gallows Tree, dozens of monkeys clutched pieces of food, clothing, bottles, and puppets.

"Pranny, my girlfriend, was supposed to meet me here," Marjormam said, as she stuffed the few supplies the monkeys hadn't stolen back into the stage. "She mustn't have seen me sleeping on the bench." The monkeys' chittering sounded like laughter. "Did you see her? A beautiful girl with short-cut blonde hair?

"I was behind the curtain," the woman said, gesturing across the square where the puppeteers were packing their supplies onto a wagon drawn by a geriatric camel. She picked up the Dread Baroness puppet and brushed dirt off her felt armor. "This is good work for an amateur. Did you make it?"

Marjormam snatched the puppet from the older woman's hands. "Pranny made that one. We planned to spend the night at the campground in Flayton. I bet that's where she's headed, don't you think?"

"I could not say," the woman said. She found a sack of boiled drake eggs behind the bench and handed them to Marjormam. "But if you need work, we are always looking for new crew."

Marjormam looked across the square at the small team of men and women wrapping up their show. She imagined Pranny and her in a few years' time, a crew of their own working for them, back in the City Infernal for three nights in Chiropractor Square. Her parents and Pranny's fathers in the audience, aglow with pride. The ovation would startle the carrion monkeys right out of their foul tree.

"She'll be in Flayton," Marjormam said, taking the eggs. The stage made an empty thudding sound when she hoisted it onto her shoulders. "She has to be. I really liked your show!"

Ghostlight chilled the city as she crossed its deserted streets. Tired manwhores called to her from beneath shaded doorways, and though they offered nothing but fleeting pleasures, they seemed to

Marjormam to be the insidious whisper of the City itself.

Why fight it? the City said. *Pranny won't be in Flayton. She's gallivanting through my streets with Seferia even now. She doesn't want you, but I do. Take your place on the spike. Stay with me.*

"She'll be there," Marjormam said to a surprised manwhore, and she ran for the City's gates. When she reached the Way of the Shrike, the impaled scolded her for running with such a heavy load on her back. How she wanted to laugh at that. Her stage was empty. Weightless.

Her toe caught an upraised cobble and she hit the Way with a crunch. The scolding calls changed to shouts of concern. Marjormam laughed in dismay. The impact had smashed the stage into a dozen jagged pieces.

The Dread Baroness puppet lay amidst the wreckage. She picked it up and carried on down the Way, but she couldn't run anymore. She tried to hold onto that image of her and Pranny returning triumphant to the City, but it seemed as unreachable as a monkey in the upper branches of the Gallows Tree.

One puppet, that's all she had left, but it was enough, wasn't it? The felt eyes of the Dread Baroness stared up at her. Good work for an amateur, the puppeteer had said. Marjormam had always thought their Dread Baroness was perfect, but the puppeteer was right: the eyes were different sizes, the black armor had been poorly stitched, and the whole thing stank of monkey shit. It was amateur garbage, just like the overly-serious play Pranny had written. No audience would ever give them an ovation, much less coin. They would starve on the road and be back in the City within weeks, begging for a post on a spike.

Without quite realizing it, Marjormam noticed she was reading the plaques at the base of each spike. 11999... 12301... 12450... As she drew closer to her spike, she found herself slowing until she stopped at number 12492. Thirteen feet of sharpened oak stood against the star-filled sky. A ladder propped on the spike invited her to climb.

Marjormam was still standing there sometime later, staring up at the spike, when Pranny called out to her, "It's not so bad as you think."

The omnibus clattered past, and there was Pranny, standing at the omnibus stop a few spikes down. At the sound of her voice, Marjormam dared to hope again, just for an instant.

But Pranny wasn't dressed for the road. She wore stockings, corset and cape, just like Seferia had been wearing, and she had a wineskin slung over one shoulder.

"Where's your girlfriend?" Marjormam said.

"She's just a friend."

"You're supposed to say that I'm your girlfriend."

"Maybe I can call you that again." Pranny unslung the wineskin and handed it

　　　THE WAY OF THE SHRIKE

to Marjormam. "The puppeteers in Chiropractor Square told me you were heading for Flayton. I'm glad you came to your senses. They call it Childhood's End for a reason."

Marjormam took the wineskin and she drank before handing it back. The stuff tasted like vinegar and it left her feeling slightly nauseated.

"Why didn't you tell me that you didn't want to go? We've been planning this for months."

Pranny squirted a bit of the wine into her mouth. "I thought you'd get over it. And I was right, wasn't I? We can still put on the show. I'll get us a gig at one of the open nights at Rind's."

Marjormam showed Pranny the filthy Dread Baroness puppet.

"Won't be much of a show."

"We'll make new ones on the weekend," Pranny said. She handed Marjormam a small tin of cream and a folded straight razor. "Rub it on the tip of the spike and your—"

"I went to the orientations," Marjormam said. She tucked the Dread Baroness puppet into her belt and took the tin and the razor. "Hold the ladder."

Marjormam started to climb. From the top of the ladder, she could see the thousands of spikepeople working their trade by ghostlight, all the way from the City's gates to the far horizon. Did she really think she was so special that she deserved something more?

Marjormam smeared cream on the tip of the spike and reached into her traveling trousers to rub it on herself. The cream left her numb. She unfolded the straight razor. Ghostlight reflected blue across the blade. Marjormam took a shuddering breath and reached between her legs to make the insertion cut.

"I'll stay through your whole shift," Pranny said. "I promise."

Marjormam was about to shut her eyes against the pain when she saw movement on the Way. Between the writhing spikepeople, a single old camel dragged a cart piled high with props and stage dressing. Pranny gazed up at her, an expectant look on her face, but the cart was drawing closer. Marjormam snapped the razor shut.

"Everything okay?" Pranny said.

"Yes," Marjormam said. "I'm done with your promises." She took the Dread Baroness puppet and drove it onto the tip of the spike, then hurried down the ladder.

"What are you doing, Marjie?" Pranny said. "You don't get paid if you don't get skewered."

"Then I won't get paid," Marjormam said. She planted a kiss on Pranny's rouged lips. "Goodbye, Pranny. Tell my parents I'll be back in a few weeks. A month at most."

Beneath the mismatched eyes of the felt Dread Baroness, Marjormam ran to join the puppeteers leaving the city.

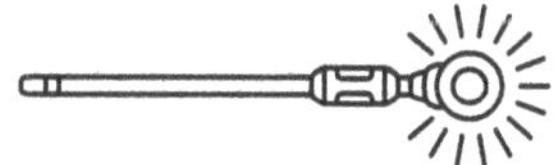

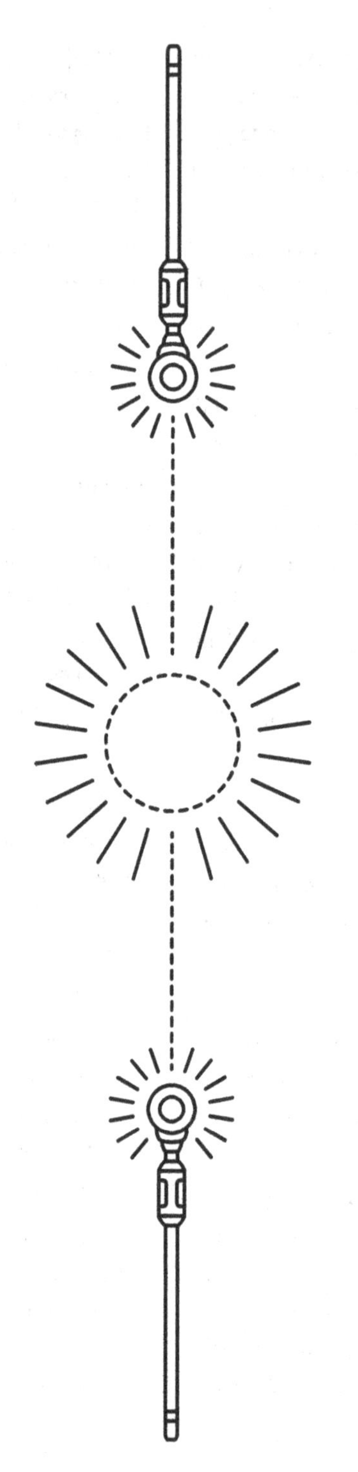

CHINAZA EZIAGHIGHALA is a physician who moonlights as a storyteller. An alumn of the University of Iowa's International Writing Program, she is published in the British Science Fiction Association's *Fission II Vol. 1* anthology, *Mythaxis* and *Brittle Paper*. CHIMERA, her debut novella, is forthcoming from Nosetouch Press in 2024. Connect with her at chinazaeziaghighala.disha.page or on twitter at @chinazaezims.

Planet Scumm conducted this interview with Chinaza via email. Some text has been lightly edited for clarity.

AUTHOR SPOTLIGHT

CHINAZA EZIAGHIGHALA

PLANET SCUMM: Does being a writer make you a better physician? If so, in what ways?

CHINAZA EZIAGHIGHALA: Being a Physician allows me the opportunity to take care of people in their most vulnerable state. When people fall ill, they come to me naked, pleading, hoping that I offer some respite. In some ways, I think that is what writing does.

People read to find respite from the world around them. They read to discover, to evolve. They plead with the author in their most vulnerable state and say, "I trust you to give me the best story experience of my life."

The question then is, will I deliver on my end? Will I give the reader that blissful experience that they seek? Being a Physician offers me no choice and I try to bring that attitude to my writing because their lives, at least in that short moment when they consume my work, are literally in my hands.

When you read fiction, do you crave more escapism or catharsis?

Both. There is always overlap for me. Some works have been so cathartic that I cry in the end. Many works. Others have helped build my imagination by expanding my mind. Most times, I just crave something I do not expect.

     CHINAZA EZIAGHIGHALA

Who are the artists and authors that most inspired you to become a writer?

Chimamanda Ngozi Adichie. She was the first writer I read who sounded like me. JK Rowling. Her Harry Potter Universe made my childhood. It opened my mind to many possibilities. Chinua Achebe. His writing reminds me that I can be my true self when writing— a philosophical Igbo thinker. Mashashi Kushimoto. He created one of my favourite characters of all time—Naruto. Eric Roth. He wrote Forrest Gump which, for reasons still unknown to me, spurred my interest in writing for film. Stephen King. *On Writing* reminds me that I just need to focus on the work and stay happy because staying happy is what matters. Neal Baer, MD. Because he makes being a Physician-Writer look so effortless. And so many others.

Your submission letter mentioned a difficult experience that inspired "A Dose of Insight." Is there any part of the real-life roots of the story you'd like to share with the reader?

I'd rather keep that private. However, it has a lot to do with the systemic healthcare issues in Nigeria. Something I hope can be rectified in the coming years.

Your debut novella comes out next year. Describe the hypothetical reader who might most fall in love with CHIMERA.

For the budding reader yet to discover their love of reading.

As a writer for the primetime series *Itura* and given your various experiences in filmmaking, can you think of any techniques or aspects of craft that prose writers could learn from screenwriters?

Prose is its own art form of course, but I think that learning to tell visual stories even in prose can make a whole world of difference for a reader. Truly engaging the senses and creating a whole new type of experience. I also think that screenwriters write great dialogue especially because people speak in real-time. Prose writers can learn how to write authentic dialogue from Screenwriters. Finally, there's a technique in Screenwriting for writing scenes where you come in late and leave early. It could be coming in halfway through a conversation or an action sequence and leaving right on/before a major climax. It builds tension and I think that can be employed in Prose as well.

AI JIANG is a Chinese-Canadian writer and an immigrant from Fujian, China. She is a member of HWA, SFWA, and Codex. Her work has appeared or is forthcoming in *F&SF, The Dark, Uncanny, Prairie Fire, Hobart Pulp, The Masters Review*— among others.

Find her on Twitter at @AiJiang_ and online at aijiang.ca.

Planet Scumm conducted this interview with Ai via email. Some text has been lightly edited for clarity.

AUTHOR SPOTLIGHT
AI JIANG

PLANET SCUMM: On average, how long does it take you to draft a short story, versus a longer work?

AI JIANG: For a short story, I'm often brewing on them for a while in my mind, but the actual writing might only take less than an hour to a few hours depending on the length of the piece. I think the short story that took me the longest to write was 5000 words spread across 2-3 days.

In terms of longer work, I've only written one novelette so far, and the initial draft of 9,000 words took me 3 days. *Linghun's* first draft took about a week, and my other novella on submission took perhaps twice that. I haven't yet finished my first novel, but at the rate I'm writing, I'd say it might take around three months or so of long writing spurts every few days. There always seems to be something else that needs attention!

What was the hardest (or easiest) piece you've written and why?

Rather than one specific piece, I'd say it's difficult for me to write sci-fi ,for the most part because I don't have a scientific background. I often have to rely on made-up science that draws inspiration from current science, so I'm always worried about how authentic it might read because the plausibility of the science I include is quite slim. But then, with how rapidly the field of science is growing, what might seem impossible today may be commonplace in the future.

Have you read anything that made you think differently about fiction?

I think there's something I can gain from everything I read, in the way that fiction can illuminate aspects of humanity, society, injustice, along with elements of craft and storytelling.

Whenever I read writers' thoughts on fiction, there is often a differentiating stance between writing for entertainment and writing "meaningful" fiction, and whenever I stumble upon these articles, they always cause me to contemplate why I myself write fiction. And I suppose my goal is a mixture of both these opinions: to write meaningful fiction that is entertaining.

Do you have any quirks or practices that get you into the rhythm to write?

I'm not sure if this would be called a quirk or practice, but I tend to procrastinate to get into the rhythm to write. As in, I will do all the tasks I could possibly do on my to-do list and exhaust the procrastination possibilities before I dive into working on a WIP. Only then can my brain focus completely on marathoning for the rest of the day.

Is there any specific piece of fiction that inspired you as you initially ventured into writing?

When I was in high school, I read many YA supernatural and paranormal books, and those definitely inspired me to want to write within those same genres. But I read many literary and SFFH classics when I entered undergrad, and I think those were the works that inspired me most when I ventured into writing seriously two and a half years ago.

What can *Planet Scumm* readers look forward to in your upcoming novellas *Linghun* and *I Am AI*?

I'm a big fan of experimentation, especially when it comes to POV use, along with exploring interesting concepts to illuminate something about our humanity and society, so I'd say that is what *Linghun* encompasses. Similarly, *I Am AI*, is very concept-driven, but it is also a reflection on the vulnerabilities and fragility of humanity, the detriments of technological reliance and replacements, along with toxic productivity.

What, or who, has been your biggest influence during your writing journey?

Writers such as Kazuo Ishiguro, Ursula K. Le Guin, Shirley Jackson, Toni Morrison, Khaled Hosseini, Virginia Woolf, among others, have definitely been some of my biggest influences—especially when I first began writing.

Currently, Odyssey Workshop has been reshaping the way that I think about the writing and pre-writing process. It has given me the tools and techniques to bring more coherency to the structuring and planning of my writing, allowing me to become more intentional and aware about my execution, and to better understand what I am trying to do with my work.

Where else can *Planet Scumm* readers find your work?

Forthcoming works include *Smol Tales Between Worlds* (a mini collection—March 2, 2023), *Linghun* (a novella—April 4, 2023), *I AM AI* (a novelette—June 20, 2023), and short stories that can be found on my website.

ON TWITTER: @AiJiang_
ON INSTAGRAM: @ai.jian.g
ON TIKTOK: @aijiang_
WEBSITE: www.aijiang.ca

Tales From Between Presents

YUME KITASEI is a Brooklyn-based Japanese and American writer of speculative fiction. Her stories have appeared, or are forthcoming in publications including *New England Review*, *Catapult*, *SmokeLong Quarterly*, *Baltimore Review*, and *Nashville Review*. Her debut novel, *The Deep Sky*, is forthcoming from Flatiron Books. She chirps occasionally @YumeKitasei.

Planet Scumm conducted this interview with Yume via email. Some text has been lightly edited for clarity.

YUME KITASEI

PLANET SCUMM: What first drew you to the science fiction genre?

YUME KITASEI: Science fiction lets you put all the things you know and take for granted—laws, societal rules, technological constraints, cultural practices—into a jar and shake them up. Sometimes, thinking about how the world *could* be can alter how you think about how the world *is*.

What is your favorite (and your least favorite) part of the writing process?

The worst part is slogging through a first draft, when you are in that time right after you thought you had a terrific idea, but what's coming out on paper doesn't match your mind's eye at all. The best part is completing a round of revision, and feeling yourself not only getting closer to where you wanted a story to be, but discovering some new things along the way too.

One of these writing processes must go: drafting, editing, or querying. Which one and why?

Querying. To write, you generally have to be committed to the act, even if no one will ever read what you write—that is never guaranteed. So you have to be okay with shouting into the void sometimes. I'd write even if I never got an opportunity to publish. I'd be sad about it, but writing is compulsion—it's just something I do.

What, if anything, was your inspiration for writing "Ghosts in the Ash"?

The story digs into how it feels to live in a place that's not your own, or that doesn't quite accept you. As someone who is biracial and bicultural, I'm not a stranger to that feeling. I've lived in four countries, and felt it in each place at some point. There's something bittersweet to it: the pleasure of connecting with other people but also the sharp loneliness of being different.

What can *Planet Scumm* readers look forward to in your upcoming novel "*The Deep Sky*"?

"*The Deep Sky*" is a feminist space thriller. It's a closed-room mystery, but also a story about finding a place to belong. Hopefully, this novel will give you a thing or two to chew on, maybe a few feels, but also a little fun.

If you could tell your younger writer self anything, what would it be?

The road may be longer than you expect, and that's okay. Don't be in a rush to publish. Spend the prelude honing your craft.

Even now that I'm published, I'm hopeful my writing will continue to improve. "*The Deep Sky*" was the fifth novel I ever wrote. I hope the sixth, tenth, twentieth I write are even better. If I ever get to twenty-five, it'll be a masterpiece.

In regards to crafting a longer work, do you prefer to plot and outline, or wing it as you go, and why?

My new strategy is to "vibe" for 20k words, outline, write to outline, then re-outline and rewrite. It's one-quarter pantsing and three-quarters plotting. I'm hoping that this more disciplined approach will leave room in the process for discovery without just chaotically thrashing around the way I used to.

Where else can *Planet Scumm* readers find your work?

Many of my short stories can be found on my website, yumekitasei.com. My debut novel, *The Deep Sky*, is available from pre-order wherever books are sold. It's out July 18 of this year.

AN INCOMPLETE INDEX OF SEMI-RELEVANT TAROT

As artists, Maura McGonagle and I both love symbology and iconography and just generally trying to capture a lot of meaning into something simple. So naturally, we threw ourselves headfirst into creating functional, thematically-appropriate tarot cards to pair with each story. When compared, we hope that cards we've designed both convey the intended meanings from the original Rider Waite deck, which influenced our compositions, as well as the underlying message of each story.

— Creative Director, Alyssa Alarcón Santo

 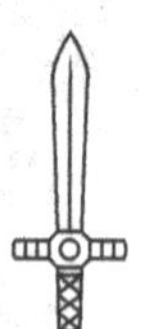   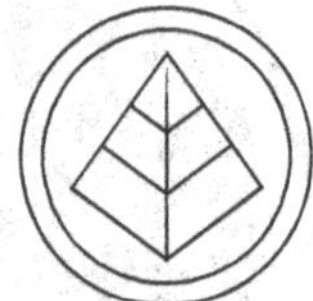

PG. VII, "ROLL ON THUNDER CHILD"

THE CHARIOT

In moments of chaos and change, the chariot presents an opportunity to shift your momentum onto a more ideal path.

↑ *Card Associations:* The Chariot symbolizes direction, willpower, and taking control. It suggests that through one's own effort, they can lead themselves to fulfillment.

↓ *Words of Warning:* Make decisions cautiously in a time of restlessness. The desire for change is strong, but ensure that your choices are from a place of logic and not impulse.

⇥ *How it Relates:* After six years of hard work and dedicated effort, longtime editor-in-chief of *Planet Scumm*, Sean Clancy, has chosen a new path, leading him forward in life but away from the Good Ship Scummy. (We'll miss you, Sean!)

THE TOWER

Things we considered foundational to our lives have come crashing down, and in that inevitable cycle of destruction and rebirth, we now have space to rebuild.

↑ *Card Associations:* The Tower symbolizes sudden upheaval and wide-scale change. It suggests old routines and existing ways of life will be upset, for better or worse.

↓ *Words of Warning:* While some change is unavoidable, some is self-initiated and changing your circumstances can come at a great cost. Understand what you will be giving up before chasing after novelty.

⇥ *How it Relates:* The city in *The Throat of San Dante* breaks itself down with the intention of rebuilding newer, better. In the process of rebuilding, it leaves destruction in its wake.

KNIGHT OF SWORDS

The knight of swords is propelled by unbridled ambition, rushing forward on a collision course with either the swells of joy or the depths of despair.

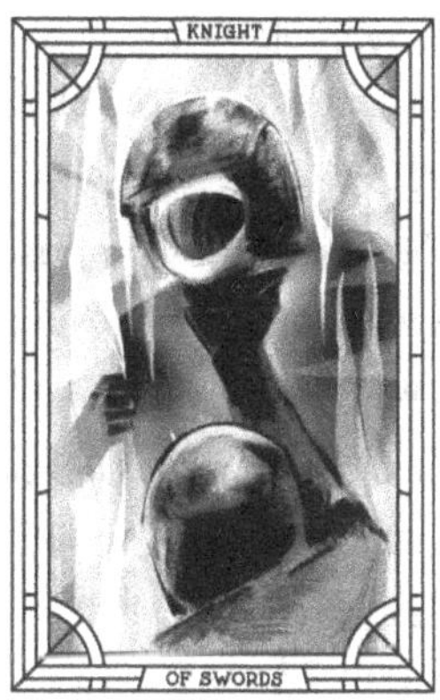

↑ *Card Associations:* The Knight of Swords symbolizes action, speed, and ambition. This figure is brave and willing to rush into battle (though their underlying motivation may be inconsistent or flawed).

↓ *Words of Warning:* If you are impetuous and take action without regard for the potential consequences, destruction is right around the corner.

⇥ *How it Relates:* Though the warrior in *After Meal* intends to remain focused on his mission, he finds himself tempted to commit terrible acts in service of his own joy.

IX OF SWORDS

Nine swords hang in the darkness, as heavy and unavoidable as the hopelessness that the subject can no longer see through.

↑ **Card Associations:** The Nine of Swords symbolizes night-mares, darkness, and anxiety. These things can be oppressive, leaving the subject feeling trapped.

↓ **Words of Warning:** The fear and despair you are experiencing may not be founded in reality. From an objective standpoint, is that feeling rational?

↠ **How it Relates:** In a hostile world, like the one in *Cover Your Eyes*, it is inevitable for the inhabitants to internalize the fear that constantly surrounds them. The protagonist finds herself haunted by the trauma of past experience.

VI OF CUPS

Even as the world rages on outside, thoughts of a once-loved home and the simpler times from childhood memory create a safe place to rest.

↑ **Card Associations:** The Six of Cups symbolizes happiness and enjoyment derived from pleasant memories. It invokes the comfort that comes with familiar people and places.

↓ **Words of Warning:** Clinging to the comforts of the past, or longing for a bygone era, prevents you from moving forward as new opportunities present themselves.

↠ **How it Relates:** The family unit in *Such Thoughts are Unproductive* is grasping at a moment long past, but despite their effort, it is slipping through their fingers. Until now, they've chosen to let memory serve as the present.

II OF CUPS

At the core of life is the transfer of energy; a current from the elements, between those that live within them, and back again to the elements.

↑ **Card Associations:** The Two of Cups symbolizes unity in partnerships, the blending of two-into-one, and reciprocity. It signals balance and understanding.

↓ **Words of Warning:** A lack of care and effort can be felt by those around you. Hardening yourself to the trials of others will ultimately hurt you as well.

⇥ **How it Relates:** The physician in *A Dose of Insight* is dispassionate to the plights of others. To spiritually right his wrong, his energy was redirected away from him, now providing the care he should have chosen to give initially.

WHEEL OF FORTUNE

The Wheel of Fortune speaks to the perpetual motion of a fluid universe, and addresses the fluctuations of human life within it.

↑ **Card Associations:** The Wheel of Fortune symbolizes an unexpected change, new conditions, and creative evolutions. It speaks to the passage of time and the myriad split paths we encounter.

↓ **Words of Warning:** An object at rest within a maelstrom will eventually be worn down by the winds of change. Flexibility requires courage but sustains less damage.

⇥ **How it Relates:** *The Battle of York* drops familiar figures into the middle of an unfamiliar quest, following an alternate path through foundational American history.

INTERPRETED BY ALYSSA ALARCÓN SANTO

VIII OF PENTACLES

When faced with the destruction of your ideal future, it will take time, diligence, and a little bit of creativity to change your fate.

↑ *Card Associations:* The Eight of Pentacles symbolizes a dedication towards creation, purposeful work, and the feeling of satisfaction that comes from achievement.

↓ *Words of Warning:* When you have no focused goal and no definable motivation, the work you do may ultimately be futile. Working from a place of intention yields stronger results.

↠ *How it Relates:* The species in *Original Home* found a way to continue on, against all odds. Through determination and perseverance, they created a new way forward.

VI OF SWORDS

A journey far from home has been slowed by the accumulation of past sorrows, but it still must be undertaken in order to move forward.

↑ *Card Associations:* The Six of Swords symbolizes a time of transition, a journey in consciousness, and the effort it takes to move on.

↓ *Words of Warning:* After periods of difficulty, it is easy to become complacent with negative feelings. The shedding of emotional baggage requires your active participation.

↠ *How it Relates:* After tragic and life-changing upheavals, the main figure in *Ghosts in the Ash* must choose to move forward with their life, even when they are surrounded by reminders of what came before.

II OF WANDS

As one changes and grows, it becomes increasingly difficult to strike the right balance between concrete thought and abstract desire.

↑ ***Card Associations:*** The Two of Wands symbolizes boldness, the courage in embarking on a new path, and the influence people have over one another.

↓ ***Words of Warning:*** It is disappointing when something begins well, but the path has become complicated by fear and suffering. Remain stubborn and push onward.

↠ ***How it Relates:*** Despite the unconventional setting of *The Way of the Shrike*, Marjormam is experiencing the familiar coming-of-age struggle between meeting expectations and her desire to choose an independent path.

AN EXTRATERRESTRIAL'S GUIDE TO BALLOON-BASED INSURANCE FRAUD

Translator's Note: This missive was given to us by our intergalactic, occasionally erstwhile ally Scummy, captain of the great pirate spacecraft that hides on the dark side of the Moon. Scummy's opinions, advice, and business practices are not endorsed by us; we're just required to share them.

Alright Alpha level investors, I have for you the quick and easy, super effective, revenue *and entertainment* generating plan you've all been waiting for: ***How to Defraud Governments of the World, Using Only A Balloon.***

No doubt you'll remember all the news stories about "mysterious balloon-based entities" being "shot down" by "governments" all around the world. I'm here today to let you in on a secret. This has *all* been a part of my latest endeavor—***an ingenious, sixty-four step plan to get rich quick***—and you now have the opportunity to join me!

Seems too good to be true, right? Are you perhaps reminded of my *wildly successful* **Cash for Pyramids** scheme? Don't worry; this new money making strategy *isn't* full of hot air—just helium!

You don't need much to get started. How about I give you a quick overview of the process before we dive into the details?

1. Permits

You'll need to acquire the intergalactic rights to your planet's exosphere, but don't worry, it's easy enough to do! Just pop over to the Galactic Department of Mechanized Vehiculation [GDMV] office near Betelgeuse and fill out the stacks of required paperwork.

2. Inventory

You'll need to supply a steady stream of balloons. Not the little ones, either. They'll need to be the rough size and shape of a StarModel X~7 Space Shuttle* to be considered a subspecies worthy of preservation. I'm sure you can estimate *exactly* how big that is and select your herd accordingly.

Translator's Note: We have no idea what this is, but we think Scummy may have built a spaceship from paper mache and tried to sell it to the Martians as a highly advanced Earth-based transportation system. That may explain why nobody from Mars calls us back anymore.

Sourcing the ideal balloon stock is easy! You just have to pander to your audience. I like to pose as the world leader of a tiny, unheard-of country with convenient access to valuable pollutants (I believe you call it dinosaur juice?). I simply offer the dino goo from one country to the leader of another big government in a trade for the proper balloons. They always think *they're* the one getting a great deal, the chumps.

3. Insurance

As you now know, your species is very good at producing balloons, but are you aware of just how valuable they can be elsewhere? Balloons are endangered on nearly *every other planet* in this galaxy. All those bleeding-heart balloon conservationists have been pumping oodles of Bjorxgx Coins™ towards preserving the natural habitats of the balloon (and I've discovered that it's pretty easy to get access to that dosh).

Now that you've gained exosphere rights and a starter collection of balloons, you'll need to get registered with the *Endangered Non-Sentient (Sometimes) Aircraft Preservation Society*, or [EN(S)APS]. Once you've been approved as a licensed balloon-tender, you can insure their habitat through [EN(S)APS], set up a sanctioned balloon breeding program, and start collecting money directly from those bleeding-heart conservationists.

4. Mobilization

Now that your operation is successfully funded, all you have to do is float your balloons through the airspace of each dumb, dumb human that controls various bits of this planet and wait for them to panic. Your practically effortless profit is in reach!

As the governments of the world start shooting down your balloons in a panicked, frenzied attempt to "defend their sovereign airspace," you can move to have them recognized as an aggressive pest in the Andromeda Solar System Registry of Species (ASSRS). Then you can finally collect your big insurance payout under the pretense of repopulating the dwindling balloon population. Bing bang boom. Easy.

A word of warning: DO NOT TRY THIS OVER ATLANTIS. Your claim will be denied since it is "technically underwater" and "mostly mythical." ** Bureaucrats, I tell you.

** Translator's Note: For real, don't anger the Atlantians. They're mad enough about the deep sea mining crew that got ahold of the giant squid's sex tape and leaked it.*

If you'd like to access the *fully detailed document* featuring all sixty-three steps of this easy-to-follow plan, subscribe to Scummy's Masterclass at any level. And remember, our Platinum Pyramid Schemers get early access to our follow-up course "**How YOU Can Both Buy AND Sell Pyramids—For Profit.**" So if you haven't already registered and made your voluntary donation of one (1) kidney, do so now!

— *That's all, Scummy out!*

TRANSLATED BY ANNA CATALANO AND LUCAS X. WISEMAN

THE PLANETS AND STARS TOTALLY INFLUENCE YOUR LIFE!

Scummy's guide to the stars, the planets, and the way the insignificant moment you exited your mother definitely, absolutely has an impact on your life (and how the planets and stars super, definitely, totally care about whether or not you ask Tony to the Spring Fling).

"Whether you're majoring or minoring in space arcana, or just really, really into big hot balls of burning plasma, pay attention to these predictions! They're definitely going to come true for most of you!"

— Scummy

☆ ☆ ☆

LEAP DAY LOSER:
FEB 29

Okay, so you're some kind of bee person, which means you're real good at following orders. I need you to go up to Alaska and launch some of my prototype pyramid balloons, ok you stupid bee? Do it! Look for the halogen glow of the afterburners and speak the following phrase aloud for entrance to my base: "Scummy really is better than every other human, and I mean that sincerely."[1]

» 1 *You don't actually have to do this. Please don't encourage him.*

AQUARIUS:
JANUARY 20 – FEBRUARY 18

A kindergartner is going to approach you and say: *"I bwoke my arm and I bit frew my lip wif my new teef,"* and if that happens, you need to immediately bow to the person to your left—they are a changeling, and this will save your life.

☆ ☆ ☆

PISCES:
FEBRUARY 19 — MARCH 20

Translator's note:

Scummy hates anybody who is a Pisces and refused to give a prediction, stating only: "they know what they did."

☆ ☆ ☆

ARIES:
MARCH 21 — APRIL 19

If you, like other Earth losers, find yourself frustrated or in want of a mate, don't wait! Don't hesitate! Just bang your head parts full speed into someone else's head parts. Such is romance, so says Scummy, who is by far an expert[2] on such matters.

» 2 *He very much isn't, and this will likely give you a concussion. But we are not medical experts.*

TAURUS:
APRIL 20 — MAY 20

You are obnoxiously stubborn, which is typical for your species, but this will serve you well for getting your way—shove any other earthlings into the dirt and achieve your dreams, no matter what they are! Your mantra should be:  [3]

» 3 Translation: "resistance is futile!"

☆ ☆ ☆

GEMINI:
MAY 21 — JUNE 21

This month, keep an eye on your evil twin, as they are not what they seem. Unless *you* are the evil twin, in which case you (much like a Pisces) know what you did...

☆ ☆ ☆

CANCER:
JUNE 22 — JULY 22

Your legs may very soon be taken from you (and perhaps doused in a gooey earth substance)—cherish them. And do summon your appendage strength to heave yourself out of whatever tin bucket you prefer to spend your days.

☆ ☆ ☆

LEO:
JULY 23 — AUG 22

Listen, your mother was right, and so was your ex. You are just a giant ball of fluff pretending to be a sentient being, not at all a ferocious predator. Don't let anyone tell you otherwise.

VIRGO:
AUG 23 — SEPT 22

Beware! Wayward witches are on the hunt for obscure and vaguely threatening rituals, and you may (definitely) be susceptible. So keep however many eyes you own fixed on anything that resembles what humans refer to as a col-dren?[4]

Additionally, avoid eating all foods.[5]

» 4 We're pretty sure he meant to say 'cauldron' here. Or... children? Unclear. He was laughing really hard.

» 5 We can't recommend taking him seriously, but hey, you do you.

☆ ☆ ☆

LIBRA:
SEPTEMBER 23 — OCTOBER 22

I don't even know with you.

Avoid, like, Jupiter or any of those other Roman gods?[6] They're all really feisty right now. And you should absolutely invest in that *thing* you're thinking about, with all your money. 100%. Right now.[7]

» 6 That's...actually good advice, so something is clearly wrong...

» 7 Oh, there it is. Yeah, don't do this.

☆ ☆ ☆

SCORPIO:
OCTOBER 23 — NOVEMBER 21

You, uh... you're good, Scorpio. You can just keep on keepin' on.

☆ ☆ ☆

   THE PLANETS AND STARS TOTALLY INFLUENCE YOUR LIFE!

So, like, this one time, I had a guy I was smuggling jars of ooze with and he told me that he was super funny—because he was a Sagittarius—and then he told really awful knock-knock jokes for the next 11 hours.[8] So don't believe everything you read... unless I wrote it, of course.

» 8 *Knock knock.*
  Who's there?
  Alpaca.
  Alpaca who?
  Alpaca the spaceship, you pack the snacks
  and let's go explore the galaxy!
  The sound of laser blasts fill the cockpit

CAPRICORN:
DECEMBER 22 — JANUARY 19

Oh, uh, you're all about... goats. Those curly horned, square eyed things with the milk? Okay. "Your goat-like determination will come in handy this week when you're climbing a steep mountain."

MARTIANS:
ANYBODY BORN ON OR AROUND
MARS

Beware Urpthxxdöx 7, and as always, beware small pecan pies. You know why.

EVEN HEROES CATCH COLDS

It was a chilly ______________ and Scummy was feeling under the
day of the space-week
weather. In a(n) ______ battle with ____________ he had lost most of his
adjective   *famous bounty hunter*
cytoplasm and caught space ______to boot! With an __________ from his
sickness   *onomatopoeia*
____, he moaned, "I guess I better see my ____________ before I lose
orifice   *medical professional*
any more of my ________."
plural organ

With a heaving sigh, Scummy ___ed himself to Comms and began to
verb
dial his rotary phone. Because Scummy saw a specialist who lived in
another star cluster, he had to dial ____ digits before the ______ voice
number   *adjective*
of Dr. ________'s receptionist addressed Scummy with an ______,"____."
alien last name   *adjective* *greeting*

"I gotta see the doc!" Scummy exclaimed. "And ____!"
adverb

"I'm sorry, we don't have anything available for _____ more _______
number   *plural unit*
_____."
of time

"Unacceptable!!" Scummy __________ "I will ___ your planet and make
verb, past tense.   *verb*
you regret the day you were _________. I will salt your fields, manipulate
verb, past tense
your __________, unleash my _________, then travel into the future and
governing official   *superweapon*
___ your descendants—"
verb

"Sir, do you think these threats are any different from the sort of ____
word
______________ I hear from the rest of Dr. ______________'s clients? This
meaning "nonsense"   *Same Alien Last Name*
kind of abuse is why no one else will ___ you."
verb

"...can I at least get a script for some space ___?"
drug